Tawny Weber
Beth Andrews

One Night with a SEAL

⬦ HARLEQUIN® BLAZE®

ISBN-13: 978-0-373-79969-5

One Night with a SEAL
Copyright © 2017 by Harlequin Books S.A.

The publisher acknowledges the copyright holders of the individual works as follows:

All Out
Copyright © 2017 by Tawny Weber

All In
Copyright © 2017 by Beth Burgoon

Recycling programs
for this product may
not exist in your area.

Printed in U.S.A.

About the Authors

Tawny Weber is the *New York Times* and *USA TODAY* bestselling author of more than forty books. She writes sassy, emotional romances with a dash of humor and believes that it all comes down to heroes. In fact, she's made her career writing about heroes, most notably her popular Navy SEALs series. Visit her on the web at tawnyweber.com. You can also find her on Facebook, Twitter, Pinterest and Goodreads.

When not writing, Romance Writers of America RITA® Award–winner **Beth Andrews** can often be found cheering on the Pittsburgh Penguins hockey team, scrolling through Instagram or reading a good book with a happy ending. Learn more about Beth and her books by visiting her website, bethandrews.net. She loves to hear from readers! You will also find her on Facebook and Twitter.

CONTENTS

Dear Reader,

I'm excited about *All Out* for a few reasons. First, Vivian and Zane were so fun to write. Sexy and challenging, they're both all about pushing themselves to get the most out of life. As a SEAL, Zane is one of the best—a fact that Vivian is thrilled to enjoy.

Another reason I'm excited about *All Out* is that this two-in-one was written with an author I admire so much, my best friend Beth Andrews. We had a great time going back and forth in the creation of these sexy twin Bennett brothers and their hot love stories.

As I finish writing my thirtieth story for Blaze, I can't believe it's been ten years since my very first book, *Double Dare*, was published by Harlequin! I've loved sharing my stories with all of you awesome Blaze readers and hope you've loved reading them just as much. Blaze is filled with fabulous stories, amazing authors and a great team at Harlequin, and while I'm so sad to say goodbye, I am excited to share *All Out* with you.

As I say goodbye, though, I'm thrilled to be saying hello to HQN Books. My SEAL Brotherhood trilogy consists of *Call to Honor*, *Call to Engage* and *Call to Redemption*. These stories have the same hot, sexy feel as my Blazes, but are bigger and filled with more emotional depth and intensity. I hope you'll check them out. I hope, too, that you'll subscribe to my newsletter at tawnyweber.com/register to hear about more new releases, great story news and to stay in touch.

Happy reading!
Tawny Weber

ALL OUT

Tawny Weber

To everyone at Blaze, those who read the books, write the books and produce the books.

Thank you for the wonderful journey.

_1_

"HASTA LA VISTA, BABY."

Sweat dripping into his eyes, Zane Bennett narrowed them enough to glare at the guy shimmying past him on the rope. He couldn't tell from behind who it was, but it didn't matter. The other man was breaking away, getting ahead.

Losing was one thing that Zane personally detested but had learned to accept when competing with fellow SEALs. After all, they were the best.

But losing to a sore winner?

Damned if that was okay.

Zane dug deep for more power. Ignoring his screaming muscles, he kicked it up from high gear to the unsustainable but kick-ass superhigh gear. Palms burning, biceps quivering, shoulders rippling, he yanked himself up his rope in three quick pulls. Rather than vaulting the wall at the top, he flipped over it, landing on the other side, double-timing it through the rest of the obstacle course to take the lead. He kept it through the three-mile run back to base, where he crossed the unofficial finish line and dropped into the sand to huff for air.

Even at eight in the morning, he was glad for the cap

that shaded his eyes from the Southern California sun as it poured its hot rays over his already sweating body.

"Nice job." The congratulations were accompanied by a slap to the back that would have felled a lesser man.

"Hey, Lansky," he greeted without bothering to look back at his senior officer. "How's it going?"

Lieutenant Jared Lansky was a SEAL and member of Poseidon, a twelve-man team deemed the elite even among the SEAL Brotherhood. A team Zane would have been breaking his ass to join if not for the fact that it was exclusive to men who'd graduated BUD/S together, all of them focused on building their reps since they'd left Basic Underwater Demolition/SEAL training with their SEAL tridents.

"Dude, why are you doing PT?" Shaking his head as if Zane had dropped a screw or two on the run, Lansky gave Zane his patented WTF look. "I thought you were on leave."

Leave.

Yeah. Two weeks without training. Two weeks without heart-pounding, muscle-building, ligament-tearing workouts. No competition, no shooting range, no testing his skills.

"My plane doesn't leave until noon." His arms resting on bended knees, Zane flicked the sand off his boots. "I figured I'd get in one last sweaty round before heading for Colorado."

"You don't sound thrilled. Problems at home?"

"Problems?" Zane laughed. His mother wouldn't allow problems. "Nah. Home is good. Really good. Two weeks of sleeping as late as I want, not shaving, eating mom's cooking? Good times, man. Time with my family, hanging out with the twin, chilling with my buds. All good."

"That's three goods. In my experience, three goods

equals bad." Jared threw up a hand before Zane could reply. "We'll get back to that. First, *the twin*?"

"My brother, Xander." Actually, thinking about seeing Xander again made the prospect of home a lot more interesting. Seeing any of his family was okay, but everything was always better when Xander was around.

"Identical?"

"Fraternal." He considered for a second, then shrugged. "But we look enough alike to pass for brothers."

"Do you have that twin mystique?" At Zane's questioning look, Jared explained, "You know, you do things alike. Think alike. Finish each other's sentences. Twin things."

"I wouldn't say that," Zane objected. Others said it a lot, but he really didn't see it himself. He doubted his brother did, either. They were themselves, not two halves of one person.

"What's your brother do?"

"He's an engineer. In the Navy." Zane slid a sidelong look and smiled. "And a SEAL."

"No shit?" Laughing in delight, Jared gave him a swift slap on the shoulder. "That's awesome. Twin SEALs. Where's he stationed?"

"Virginia."

"The two of you ever serve together?"

"Nope. I enlisted the day after we turned eighteen. He went the Annapolis route after graduating high school. My focus was explosive ordinance, his was engineering."

"Is he the reason you blew through OTC like there was a tiger on your ass?"

"Nope." He had gotten his bachelor's degree and went through officer training in the shortest amount of time possible, but it had nothing to do with keeping up with Xander. "I simply wanted to beat Cole Hanes. I pretty much forgot about the guy after we went our separate ways when

I kicked his butt in BUD/s. Word got back to me that he was talking smack about me. That once he made officer, he'd prove once and for all who was the better SEAL."

"So rather than accepting that nothing could take away from graduating top of your BUD/s class, you busted ass, tripled your workload to get your degree then plowed through OTC in record time all because some idiot was trying to make himself look good?" Lansky slanted him that WTF expression again. "Why?"

"He challenged me." Zane shrugged. "A challenge is just a fancy-ass dare, isn't it? And only a wimp walks away from a dare."

"True that," Lansky agreed, his boyish looks contemplative as he stared out at the ocean. They sat in silence for a few seconds, then he sighed.

"We're hard-wired to compete. To push, to be strong, to be the best. That's why we are the best." He waited for Zane's grin before continuing, "But sooner or later, you realize that the only person you have to prove anything to is yourself. Once you're comfortable with that, you can pick and choose the dares you care about. Makes life easier."

Zane nodded. He got that, he really did. But…

"'The only easy day was yesterday,'" he quoted the oft-used SEAL phrase.

"There you go." Lansky gave a rueful laugh. "I suppose that's why going home is so *good* that you say it three times? Because you're worried you'll lose your edge?"

"Please, my edge is permanent," Zane said dismissively. "It was carefully and strategically honed in the deceptively picturesque town of Little Creek, Colorado. A place where everybody knows everybody else and minding the neighbors' business is a way of life."

"Sounds nice."

"Sounds boring as hell," Zane acknowledged. "Which

is why we started issuing challenges. Dares, if you will. For the craziest crap. Who could jump farthest off the high school gym roof? Who could eat the most little green apples before competing in the track meet? Who looked best in a dress and heels?"

"Beg pardon?" Lansky interrupted, with a raised eyebrow.

"Halloween, junior year of high school," Zane explained before continuing his recital of various dares and challenges. "And every trip home, it continues."

"Is that the cause for all those *goods*? You want to avoid the dares-slash-challenges?" Lansky gave him a pitying head shake. "Way to represent the team, Bennett."

"Once you've rappelled out of a helicopter into the Atlantic during a storm while a gang of Somali pirates are shooting at you, being challenged to chug-a-lug a dozen Big Gulp slushies just isn't the same."

Although the brain-freeze threat was a hazard that couldn't be dismissed.

"So don't play."

"Yeah, right." Zane laughed. "Like you said, we're hardwired to compete. I can't walk away from a challenge. Ever."

"You might want to work on that."

"Might."

But probably not on this trip. This trip would come with plenty of challenges. He was heading back for a high school reunion and the gang would be all there. But after ten years, most of the guys he'd gone to school with were settled down. Living the nine-to-five life with wives and, in some cases, kids even.

Talk about challenges. How the hell did they do that? It was the complete opposite of his motto: No Ties, No Lies.

"You ever worry that we live so far over the edge that we aren't suited to, you know, regular life?"

"You said it yourself. We're not meant for regular life, Bennett. But like picking and choosing our challenges, we have to learn to decompress from time to time or we'll burn out." Lansky's voice tightened, his eyes locked on the churning waves as if searching for some answer only the ocean could offer. "You know as well as I do that the body needs time between workouts for the muscle fibers to mend. If you want to stay sharp and last the duration, you take advantage of those valleys between each peak."

"Peaks and valleys, huh?"

"Yep." With that and another slap to the back, Lansky got to his feet. "You can always try my tried-and-true method of resting."

"Chasing women?"

"Works every time," Lansky shot back with a laugh before sauntering across the sand to join the other men.

Zane stayed where he was. After all, he wasn't on duty. He was heading for that valley called home.

He'd just have to find something interesting to keep his senses alert, his skills challenged and his body honed.

Maybe Lansky had it right.

Maybe he'd have to find himself a woman.

2

"WOW. NOW, THAT'S A PENIS."

Humming as she gave said penis a careful inspection, Vivian Harris finally straightened and offered a satisfied smile.

"It does look good, doesn't it?" Noting it was a smidge uneven, she sprinkled a hint more glitter on the right side to bring out the curve. "I think it might be my best work yet."

"Absolutely, amazingly edible," Minna Karter said, her brown eyes as round as her glasses. When she wet her lips, looking as if she wanted to kneel down and give it a good lick, Vivian quickly grabbed a hot pink lid and fitted it in place.

"Your favorite triple-chocolate fudge cake layered with Bavarian cream and covered in modeling chocolate." Vivian put a snappy black bow on the box, adding the darling bakery sticker she'd printed on her inkjet claiming the confection was made with love at The Sweet Spot. "Guaranteed to keep your bridal shower guests happy."

"They're going to love it, Viv. I am blown away at how great this looks. I'll bet nobody's ever seen one this gorgeous."

"A cake, or a penis?"

"Tough choice," Minna said, laughing, "but I meant the cake. You're really rocking this new sideline of yours. I mean, I'd have ordered a cake from Little Creek Bakery no matter what, since it's your family's. But…"

"But they only make regular, boring, round—or if they're really wild, square—cakes here," Vivian agreed with a nod. "I've been asking them for years to branch out, to widen the offerings, but noooo."

She rolled her eyes at her family's narrow-minded refusal.

"Which would be why I'm picking this up after-hours when nobody else is around?"

"It wouldn't have been a big deal." At Minna's pointed stare, Vivian admitted, "My parents are out of town for the week so I'm in charge of the bakery. I was able to bake and decorate it here instead of at home."

"You'd think they'd be a little more open to expanding their offerings."

"Not everyone likes the idea of their only daughter molding phallic symbols out of cake."

"You do more than that," Minna objected. "You made that pair of songbirds for Lana's birthday, you did the mermaid for Josie's daughter, and you even did that Harley for your brother's birthday. Never mind all the other cakes and confections you're selling off your website."

Minna shook a chastising finger before Vivian could shrug that off—and since by her calculations, she wasn't yet earning half what she'd need to support herself, it really was shrugworthy.

"You're living the dream, remember," Minna reminded her in fervent tones.

Vivian had discovered a series of books called *Living the Dream!* written by Lola Bean. They focused on arranging wishes, hopes and goals into definable dreams and had inspired her like crazy. She'd read all of the books, then worked through the quizzes, study guides and questionnaires, narrowing down random ideas and what ifs into actual life goals built on a dream that touched her heart.

Vivian considered herself an artist. One who honored sexuality and the human form. But she couldn't draw or paint, and try as she might, she couldn't write a decent story. So, through Lola's first course, "Finding the Dream that Makes You Sing," she'd combined her two talents, sensual art and baking, and created The Sweet Spot.

As Lola so often said, with the power of that much emotion behind her dreams, how could she fail to build her dream life? And she was right. It'd given Vivian focus for the first time in twenty-four years. A sense of empowerment and excitement over building her dream career.

What it hadn't done was actually give her that career. Yet.

Vivian wasn't giving up, though.

After reading through the entire booklist, joining Lola's newsletter and finding her on social media, Vivian had been thrilled when the woman had opened group coaching. She'd convinced Minna, their friend Lisa and Lisa's sister, Corinne, to do the coaching with her and, wow, talk about results.

Thanks to Lola's advice, after six years of dating, Minna was finally marrying the man of her dreams. Lisa had gone back to school to get her degree and Corinne—well, Corinne's dreams kept changing. She wasn't quite the dream success story, which was fine with Vivian since it made her own mediocre success look better.

"Don't look so bummed," Minna chided, obviously reading her expression. "You're great at what you do."

As if to prove it, Minna whipped off the lid and showed off the penis again, complete with a sweep of one hand.

"It does look good, doesn't it," she murmured. "But I'm still not quite living the dream."

Vivian's goal was to be the go-to gal for sexy cakes and candies. She specialized in clever, sculpted, suggestive treats of all sorts. It didn't have to be overt, like the sparkling penis. She loved getting that hint of sex across black lace formed from royal icing or leather from modeling chocolate. She'd created everything from an orgy of cupcakes to a madam's cake—a four-layer devil's food cake covered in black "leather" with red lace and sugar whips.

And while she was doing okay, she hadn't quite found the key to success yet. She was pretty confident of her skills, and was sure her prices were right. And she'd built a great online store. It was just a matter of getting people to check it out and buy.

"Did you hear anything from that program you'd applied to?"

The program was an internship with one of the most respected dessert culinary programs in the country. If accepted, she'd be spending a year studying under Geoffrey of Decadence Desserts. Learning the ins and outs, not only of perfecting her dessert-making skills, but also business and marketing knowledge that'd help her build The Sweet Spot into *the* name in sensual treats.

The problem was, the internship took place in California. So it not only included moving away from her hometown, but leaving her comfy job working for the family bakery. Sure, she hated the tedious repetition of making the same desserts over and over. And she was so over her family's disdain for her creative choices of sensual cake decor. But it was home and it was a job and, well, it was safe.

She'd been excited when she'd applied. All hopped up on one of Lola's inspirational lessons on chasing the dream. But now? California meant giving up her comfort for a low-paying job living in a dorm with a bunch of strangers. Vivian just wasn't sure it was worth it.

"No word yet," was all she said, though.

"You'll get there," Minna assured her quietly as she covered the cake again. "You know Lola says you're holding yourself back. You're not fully committing."

Vivian had to clench her teeth to keep from arguing. Not because she disagreed. But she'd argued this point so many times that she simply couldn't stand to hear that she had to give up her safety net again.

"I'll get there," was all she finally said.

Looking relieved at the response, Minna said, "I know you will," then changed the subject.

After assuring her that she'd come up with something fun for shower favors, Vivian waved her friend out of the bakery. As soon as Minna was gone, she grabbed her iPad and opened up her website.

Maybe she needed to do more advertising? Vivian slid through the samples, her smile growing as she looked at each one. Granted, there were more sketches than actual photos. Mostly because she hadn't scored a lot of orders yet and she couldn't justify making a slew of baked goods just to take photos. But picture or sketch, they all looked great.

If she did say so herself.

The infamous penis cake, perfectly proportioned—to an eight-foot-tall man, granted—with a glistening flesh-colored modeling-chocolate covering and any variety of fillings.

Bikini cupcakes, each breast covered in sassy polka dots with just a hint of cherry-gel nipples peeking through the lace.

Three-dimensional bodies—both male, female and a few with both—made not from Rice Krispies Treats like some bakers used, but delicious cake through and through.

She should be a huge success.

The only problem was that she worked at her parents' bakery and they weren't a fan of her dreams. Which wouldn't be a big deal except this was their store, as they'd snippily pointed out just last week. And apparently paying for the ingredients she used didn't make up for using their space with her crazy ideas and wicked creations.

Vivian sniffed her disdain, but since she hadn't found any way around that particular issue yet, she had to admit it did play into Lola questioning the seriousness of her commitment. According to her, Vivian should walk away from the family business and focus on her own. Dreams required risk, chapter twelve. Safety nets only slowed progress.

"Shouldn't you be working?"

Breath knotted in her chest, Vivian spun around, almost falling on her butt thanks to her four-inch heels and slim pencil skirt.

"Mike," she said, one hand pressed against her chest to keep her heart from leaping out. "What're you doing here?"

Having obviously used his key to the back door, her brother stood in the pass-through between the storefront and the kitchen, frowning. Older by three years and their parent's perfect child, Mike strode behind the counter to look over her shoulder.

"Why are you messing around with that stuff again? More of your dirty cakes and crazy ideas? C'mon, Viv, give it up and focus on the work you're paid for," he nagged in that big-brotherly tone that made his disdain for any other work she did clear.

Fingering the fifty in the pocket of her ruffled apron, Vivian debated waving it under his nose. But she knew it was pointless. Like their parents, Mike considered Vivian's side job to be a silly little hobby, something they hoped she'd give up soon. Preferably before too many people learned of it and made the connection between Little Creek Bakery and its three generations of boring baked goods and The Sweet Spot, with its naughty selection of edible treats.

"Shouldn't you be dressed like an uptight banker?" she asked, giving his casual jeans and button-down shirt a smirk.

"Shouldn't you be dressed more, I don't know, like someone who works in a bakery instead of a forties movie star?"

"You think I'm pretty enough to be a movie star?" Vivian teased, adding a sassy smile to her hair toss because she knew it'd bug him. The only thing more irritating than her brother's criticism of her side business was his critique of her vintage style.

"I think you're too much a handful as it is for me to answer a question like that." As he spoke, Mike went through the bakery case, filling a standard pink cardboard box with a selection of choice cookies, brownies and muffins.

"What are you doing here? I'm pretty sure our parents left me in charge of the bakery while they're on yet another vacation." Vivian glanced at the clock to make sure she hadn't lost time somewhere. "And since I am, shouldn't you be bossing your tellers around at the bank instead of bugging me?"

"Shouldn't you be closing out the cash register and prepping for tonight's baking instead of playing on your computer?"

"Playing?" Vivian made a show of tapping one crimson fingernail on her iPad, opened it to her website and flipped through a few more cake images. "The register is already closed out, so whatever you're taking there will have to be paid with exact change."

"Cute," he said, closing the box. "Here," he said, waving a piece of paper. "I brought you a special order. Desserts for the class-reunion welcome reception."

Vivian looked at the order and congratulated herself for holding back a sigh. *Booooring*, she thought, running one long nail down the list.

Simple vanilla cookies. Plain frosted cupcakes. Six-dozen standard petit fours. *Yawn, yawn, yawn*. And one three-tier cake in the high school colors, complete with a sugar photo of the school mascot, a roaring panther.

"You know, I could make the entire cake in the image of the panther," she suggested. "Dress him up just like the mascot, complete with a Pikes Peak High pennant."

"Stick with the sugar photo." He started writing up a list of what he'd boxed, then pulled out his wallet. "I'll pick it all up on Sunday afternoon, save you the delivery."

"Sunday? You're only giving me three days warning? I have other orders, Mike. A Saturday wedding, four birthday cakes and a croquembouche for Mrs. Fiore's daughter's shower. With the parents gone, I'm the only baker here."

"You can handle it. Bring in more counter help if you have to," he said with a shrug, handing her a ten and four ones.

"What? You're not helping? I have to make this entire boring, cookie-cutter order by myself?" She glanced over it again. There wasn't a sparkle of edible glitter or even a shiny cherry anywhere to be found.

"Use your imagination," Mike said, giving her an encouraging look. "Pretend it's fun."

Vivian knew there was no doubt they were related. The Harris genes bred too strong, with their flaxen hair— although Vivian's was a shoulder-length sweep fashioned in the classic forties style. Their huge brown eyes—but Vivian made sure hers looked even larger with heavy black liner that accented her lush lashes. And their tall, broad-shouldered build—Vivian's being a lot more feminine than her former-football-playing brother and complete with generous curves.

But she'd long ago accepted that they were only similar in looks.

"You're in charge of the bakery, you figure it out. I'll be busy celebrating having all my pals home."

All his pals?

A thrill of delight shot through her.

"The Bennett brothers are coming home?"

"Yep, Xander and Zane should be here " Mike looked at his watch and grinned "—within the hour."

"Both of them?" At her brother's scowl, Vivian made a show of sweeping her long blond bangs away from her face and giving him a wide-eyed look of concern. "Are you sure Little Creek can handle an invasion by the Bad Boy Bennetts?"

"Probably not," Mike replied with a laugh. "Luckily they're only here for ten days. Other than breaking a few hearts, I don't think they can do much damage with so little time."

"Last time they were only home a week and they got into a huge bar fight after you challenged them to see who could drink the most shots. They broke the table at the diner arm wrestling and, if rumor is correct, they were seen streaking down Main Street at three in the morning as part of some insane decathlon." Oh, how she'd wept over missing that sight.

"Nah, the streaking was just a rumor. But the rest is true." Mike's grin widened. "I'm going to have to do some serious thinking if I'm going to top all of those challenges."

Vivian had a few challenges she wouldn't mind offering Zane. Talk about a dream worth living—if only for ten days.

Her fingers tapping a beat over the boring order form, Vivian gave herself a minute to delve into her favorite fantasy. The one that starred her and Zane Bennett covered in nothing but chocolate frosting and a few tempting dollops of whipped cream.

Maybe it was time to try out a few of those coaching lessons on something other than business. After all, if she could make a glistening penis-shaped cake worthy of oohs and aahs, how hard could it be to get her hands on Zane Bennett's real one?

Vivian flashed a wicked smile.

Hopefully, once she got her hands on it it'd be very, very hard.

3

WONDERING IF A person could go stir-crazy in less than eight hours, Zane parked his Harley in front of Myer's Pub. Tugging off the helmet, he automatically checked the vicinity.

It looked pretty much like it had all his life.

The buildings, businesses and signs were the same. He recognized a number of the cars parked along the street, along with quite a few of the dozen people going about their business. The bakery across from the pub had a new striped awning, but that appeared to be about it for changes.

He'd spent the afternoon visiting family, and now he was ready to see friends. That ought to liven things up a little, Zane decided as he strode into the bar. One of the reasons he always opted to stay with his bud Lenny instead of at the family home was the freedom to enjoy whatever fun he found here at Myer's.

He was ready for some fun.

He was also early.

No problem. He was sure he'd find plenty to entertain him until the old gang arrived. Lansky's advice ringing in his ears, he scoped out the action. The bartender was familiar, but not in a did-I-do-her kind of way.

"Quinn? Quinn Oswald, right?" He recognized the slim brunette from high school. They hadn't run in the same circles, but everyone who attended Pikes Peak High recognized their Princess. And clearly, the years were kind to royalty. With her dark hair waving around a pretty face, Quinn made a black tank and jeans look damned good. "I didn't realize you'd moved back to town."

"There's no place like home," Quinn quipped with a flash of a smile. "After all, where else does a girl have a chance to award both of the Bennett brothers the honor of being Pikes Peak High's most valuable graduates?"

"You're handing out the award, huh? Guess that's one way to get us up on stage."

"You don't seem thrilled."

Thrilled at the idea of getting up on stage to receive an award he didn't want for classified work he did in a job he preferred no recognition for?

Obviously seeing the reluctance on his face, Quinn leaned across the bar to offer in a husky voice, "I'll be presenting it in a very sexy little dress, if that helps."

"I can't think of much a sexy little dress doesn't help," Zane said, grinning as he leaned on the counter and gave her a once-over. "Are you handing out hugs and kisses with that award?"

"I could be," she teased. Before she could say more, the other bartender, a hulking blond with a nearly invisible goatee harrumphed and gave her a get-back-to-work look.

Quinn rolled her eyes at the guy's back, but did put the flirting away to give Zane a cheerful smile.

"In the meantime, what can I get you to drink?"

"Negra Modelo." Looking around, he pointed toward the prime spot in the back next to the pool table. "Make it two. And a pitcher of Bud."

"You're that thirsty?" Then her big blue eyes widened. "Or is your brother joining you?"

"You look worried," he said with a laugh. "Don't be. I'll keep him in line."

"But who's going to keep you in line?" she teased, handing him the first of the two beers to take with him.

"Why ask the impossible?" he shot back with a wink, tucking a five into the oversized glass mug next to the register.

Zane made his way to the table in a flurry of greetings, a few backslaps and one intriguing offer from a woman he remembered as having amazing flexibility. A scowling redhead walking out of the back room caught his attention as he slid into the chair facing the doors.

"Hey there, Dianne," he greeted the bar owner, noting the older woman was looking as badass as ever with that narrow-eyed expression of warning. "How's it going?"

"Well, well, if it isn't one of the Bad Bennett Brothers," she returned with sharp smile, casting a cautious look over the crowd. Scouting for troublemakers, he figured. "I heard you boys would be in town. I figured you'd hit my place."

"Nowhere better to go for a good time."

"Where's Xander?"

"How do you know I'm not Xander?" he said with a wink.

"First, you've got that scruffy thing going on, and everyone knows that Zane hates to shave and does so as little as possible when he's on leave." She ticked one finger in the air. "Second, of the two of you, Xander's the gentleman."

He was? Zane arched one brow. What the hell did that make him?

"And third, of the two of you, Xander watches patiently while Zane always looks like he's about to pounce." Three fingers in the air, she paused to give him a wide-eyed smirk. "Well?"

"Well," Zane said, folding his hands behind his head as he leaned the chair back to rest on the rear legs, "I think it's safe to say that we've lost our mystique around these parts."

"Oh, don't worry about that." Dianne patted his shoulders. "There's plenty of mystery left. Enough to intrigue any number of women in town. I'm sure there'll be a long line of them thrilled to enjoy some of that mystery you spread around. Just don't be starting fights in my bar."

"Yes, ma'am," he murmured as she walked away.

Tipping back his beer, he pondered his lack of enthusiasm over spreading mystery. He liked—no, actually he loved—exchanging orgasms with all manner of single ladies. Tall ones, short ones, sassy ones, intense ones. His only hard-and-fast rule other than their being single was to keep the exchanges to one night—or in extreme circumstances, maybe an entire weekend.

But there was something about the idea of women lining up, just waiting. Where was the thrill in that?

He sucked down the rest of his beer, wishing it'd wash away the taste of dissatisfaction.

"Bennett!"

"Harris," Zane greeted, shoving to his feet to wrap one arm around the other man's shoulder and giving him a thump on the back. "Check you out. Mr. Big Shot bank manager, Little League coach and, what did I hear? You're running for the city council?"

"You forgot head of the reunion committee," Mike said, dimples flashing as he grinned. "Dude, you really should think about stepping it up and doing something for your community."

"You really should think about kissing his butt," injected Kyle Daley as he joined them. "Like a SEAL needs your advice on anything besides how to pick out a tie?"

"The only advice you have is how to look pretty," Mike shot back as Zane greeted Kyle with the same back-thumping hello.

"Yo, Zane," Joe Beck called out as he wove his way through the thickening crowd. "About time you came back to entertain us."

"Where's Xander?" Kyle asked, grabbing a chair with one hand, gesturing for a beer with the other.

"He'll be here. What about Lenny?" Zane wondered, looking around for the last member of the group of guys he and Xander had run with since grade school. "I thought he was joining us."

"He'll be here. He got stuck working the afternoon shift at the gas station."

"What happened to his job at the power plant?"

"Lost it." Joe grimaced as he pulled up his own chair. "His old lady kicked him out, too. He's renting that apartment over the bakery, trying to get back on his feet."

"Over the bakery? I thought your sister lived up there." Zane shot a look at Mike, whose parents owned the bakery.

"She does, but there are two apartments up there." Mike shrugged. "This way Lenny's got a place he can afford and Viv isn't on her own."

"Still playing overprotective big brother? Aren't you worried about letting a dog like Len loose around your baby sister?"

The three men laughed, Mike's sounding a little forced.

"Lenny's scared of Vivian," Kyle explained. Before he could elaborate, Zane's brother sauntered into the pub. As the others called out greetings, Zane eyed his twin.

Yeah, he could see why Dianne claimed Xander was a gentleman. Nobody would mistake them for brothers, but while Xander looked just as capable of kicking serious ass, he was approachable. And approach they did, especially the women.

Relaxing now that his back was covered, Zane started on his second beer and prepared to have a good time. Life was always good when Xander was around.

An hour and two pitchers of beer later, the six of them had commandeered the pool table. Par for the course, the insults were flying right along with the laughter.

"Whew, I'd like to take her out," Lenny said, watching a stacked blonde saunter past them toward the ladies' room. "She's turned me down four times, though. But she's giving you the do-me look, Xander. You gonna go for it?"

Xander glanced over, noted the hot inspection the blonde was giving him and the invitation in her eyes, then turned back to the pool table.

"Nope. Zane went out with her a few years ago."

"So?"

"Bennett brothers don't share," Joe reminded the others. "Remember? Any chick one of them does—dates, I mean," he corrected at Xander's arch look, "is on the other's do-not-touch list."

"Is that why the two of you live on opposite coasts? To keep the field clear for the other?"

"No. It's so we can spread the joy of the Bennett brothers around. Our little favor to womankind," Zane joked.

"Methinks it's challenge time," Kyle said, draining his fourth beer and reaching for the pitcher.

"Haven't you grown up yet?" Xander asked, his attention on the table as he executed a wicked bank shot.

"C'mon, it's tradition."

"He's got a point," Kyle remarked from his position at the table, feet propped on an empty chair as he waited to play the winner. "We've been issuing challenges since second grade when Joe dared the two of you to jump off the dugout to see who could land closest to the pitcher's mound."

"Or Mike's cookie challenge. The one where Xander beat you by eating four-dozen snickerdoodles."

"Four dozen and two," Xander corrected from the pool table. "Zane upchucked at forty-nine."

"Drag racing on Old March Road."

"Who could catch the most bass when we camped at Adobe Creek."

"Who could get the most applause singing 'Living on a Prayer' in the cafeteria."

Zane exchanged an eye roll with his brother, amused at the replay of some of their stupider dares over the years. The raw-egg one had definitely been vile.

"I think we've outgrown being dumbasses," Zane decided, getting to his feet as Xander made his last shot to win the game.

"We can't have a reunion without a challenge," Mike objected.

"And I've got the perfect one," Joe claimed, returning to the table with another pitcher of beer and a grin. "Remember the girl everyone wanted to date in school?"

"No," Zane said. He'd dated pretty much all the girls he wanted. Then he saw Xander's gaze shift toward the bar. Following it, he frowned. "You mean the Princess?"

"Yep, the Princess. Quinn Oswald was the finest girl in our class. Nobody here scored with her then, and nobody's scored with her since she moved back to Little Creek." From Joe's expression that wasn't for lack of trying on his part.

Tension shot off Xander like bullets from a gun. Nothing pissed him off more than seeing someone disrespecting a lady.

"We don't bet on sex," Zane said, laying one hand on

All Out

Xander's arm before he could throw the punch his scowl promised was coming.

"Not sex," Joe said, backing up with his hands in the air. "A date. Just a date."

"To the reunion dance," Kyle added. "Last night of the event, everyone's wearing clothes. Nothing rude about that, right? It'll be like prom night all over again."

If Zane recalled, there had been a lot of *not* wearing clothes on prom night. But maybe that'd just been him and Cait Carson.

"Just a date?" Xander asked in a chill tone, despite the tension Zane still felt shooting off him.

"A date with Quinn Oswald to the reunion dance. Let's make it easy on her and keep the choice between the two of you." Mike looked from Xander to Zane and back again. "Challenge issued."

The brothers' eyes met.

There was something in Xander's that Zane couldn't read. He hesitated, but didn't ask. Not here in front of everyone.

"It's better than raw eggs," he pointed out instead.

"Yeah." Brow creased, Xander looked across the room at Quinn again. "Sure. Why not."

"Challenge accepted," Zane said after a second, his eyes still on his brother's face. Something was definitely up. But he knew he wouldn't get anything out of Xander that Xander didn't want to share.

Zane grinned. He'd make him share later.

For now, he had a pool game to win.

And win he did, playing all comers over the next hour. He'd just accepted Lenny's tequila challenge, and the offer of the guy's couch since it meant Zane only had to walk across the street instead of driving, when Kyle sidled up next to him.

"Dude, Xander is getting a step up on you," Kyle muttered, adding an elbow to the ribs as emphasis.

Zane glanced over to see his brother at the bar with the Princess and shrugged.

"There's plenty of time," he said, grabbing his shot glass and toasting Lenny. "And fair's fair. Xander got there first, it's his shot."

Zane was drinking his.

But Zane's thoughts weren't on the challenge, the reunion or even sexy princesses when he walked out of the bar. Not at closing, as he'd figured, but at half-past ten. Because, apparently, everyone had to work in the morning.

What the hell?

Wondering when they'd all gotten so old, he turned into the alley between the bakery and the coffee shop, heading for the stairs that led to Lenny's place.

And rammed into a wall.

A tall, blond, curvaceous wall that cussed like a sailor when her feet went flying out from beneath her.

"Sorry," he muttered, making a grab and catching only fabric. He snagged her arm at the last second, holding her there, teetering on high heels.

Whoa.

His smile spread wide and wicked at the sight of the gorgeous blonde. She looked like a forties movie star with her side-swept bangs, sloe eyes and Cupid's-bow lips. She didn't look happy, though.

Probably because he'd ripped her blouse, leaving her standing in a body-skimming black skirt that hit her shapely knees, stiletto heels and, if the dangling fabric was any indication, a lace demi-cup bra.

"Hello, gorgeous."

4

"WHAT THE HELL?" Vivian cursed, yanking herself free from the jerk that'd rammed into her.

One arm pinwheeled as she tried to keep her balance, the other clutching the box of her latest creations close to her chest. For one second, she thought she had a chance as the stiletto heel of her sandal found cement.

But she was no match for gravity.

She hit the ground.

The box hit the air.

It rained chocolate. Freshly molded confections flew high in the air before gravity brought them down, too. Squealing, Vivian threw out her hands, trying to catch as many as she could from her prone position.

"Don't let them—" she huffed "—hit the ground."

Groaning as they did just that, Vivian dropped three pieces she'd rescued into her lap, then shoved at the hair curtaining her face. The better to glare as she cursed the man who'd knocked her on her ass.

That was when she got a good look at him.

Oh.

Vivian's breath caught in her chest. She was pretty sure

there was some surprise mixed in there, but mostly what was running through her system was pure lust.

"Zane? Zane Bennett?"

"Damn, sorry about that."

He didn't sound sorry, though.

He didn't look it, either.

He looked sexy. So, so sexy.

Those dark eyes, the chiseled jaw and, oh, baby, that bad-boy smile of his. It was enough to melt what was left of Vivian's chocolate.

"Hi," she breathed as he helped her to her feet. Realizing she sounded—and probably looked—like a wide-eyed groupie, she cleared her throat and found her pride. "It's great to see you again."

"Do we know each other?" he asked, his eyes narrowed as if he were trying to remember where from. Vivian bit her lip instead of answering. She didn't want him seeing her as Mike's little sister. Something about that designation had always seemed to make her invisible in the past. And invisible was the last thing she wanted to be around Zane.

So she took a deep breath, thrust out her breasts and offered her sexiest smile.

"We've never actually been introduced," she said truthfully. "But everyone in town knows who the Bennett brothers are."

"Is that so?" he murmured, his voice dropping one sexy decibel.

"That's so." Vivian cocked her hip to one side and lifted one hand to tick them off, one by one. "The Bennett brothers facts. Twins. SEALs. Football heroes reputed to have scored even more off the field than on."

His grin widened.

"The Bennett brothers can never refuse a dare, never

back down from a challenge. Xander holds the Little Creek RBI record, but you, Zane, won three pink slips racing your Chevelle on Old Marsh Road. Nobody has ever broken your doughnut-eating record, but one of this year's graduates got within touching distance of taking Xander's role as chug-a-lug champ."

"As always, our reputation precedes us." His laugh faded into a wince as he looked at the mess at their feet. "I've got to say, this is the first time I've plowed into a gorgeous woman so hard that she lost her…" He glanced down again with a frown. "Is that candy?"

Sexy-lingerie bridal shower candy, as a matter of fact.

At her silence, he knelt down to help her gather her ruined chocolate. After scooping up a few, he glanced at them and laughed.

"Is this a bikini top?"

Actually, it was a bra. It went with a thong. Vivian bit her lip to keep from blurting that out.

"Sure," she said, since bikini was easier to explain than lingerie to a gorgeous man who made her breathless with need. Vivian scooped fast, snagging tiny chocolate nighties, baby dolls and corsets. It wasn't that she didn't want Zane to see her undies, but maybe not here on the street.

"I had no idea Little Creek Bakery was quite so imaginative," he said, grabbing another piece, lifting it high to see the details in the streetlights. "Whoa, is this a garter belt?"

Hoping the cloak of night hid her embarrassment, Vivian wet her lips and fought the urge to grab the candy out of his hands.

"How many styles have you got here?" he wondered, bending down to scoop up another handful. Instead of tossing them into the box like she was, though, he took time to inspect every one of them. "I'm impressed. There might be some here I didn't know existed until now."

Yeah, right. She was willing to bet that Zane Bennett knew just about everything there was to know about women's sex wear.

"If rumors are anything to go by, though, you have plenty of personal experience to call on. Maybe I should ask you for advice for my next batch?"

"Sweetheart, I wrote the book," he teased. "You want suggestions, I'm your man."

Vivian was proud of herself. Her breath only shuddered a little and she managed to keep her moan of delight in her head.

"So what's the deal?" He lifted another piece of candy, this one a little bigger than the others, and frowned. "A chocolate homage to Victoria's Secret?"

"They're an experiment," she explained. "Um, there's this bridal shower and after making the cake, I had this idea for party favors."

"And I ruined them," he realized, not looking the least bit sorry. "Guess you'll have to make another batch. You want help?"

Oh.

Vivian's mind went blank. Mouth dry and heart racing, she could only stare. She wanted to think there was a double entendre in that offer, but the dim light wasn't enough to judge his expression.

"Do you have any experience?" She waited a beat, long enough for his eyes to meet hers. The look in those dark depths made her want to squirm. *Oh, yeah.* He had plenty of experience. She took another moment to steady herself before adding, "With making chocolate?"

"Making…chocolate?" He smiled suggestively. "What do you think?"

Oh, God.

She tried to come up with a witty comeback. Or, hell, she'd settle for a lame one if she could just get the words out of her mouth. But how was she supposed to think with all this lust pounding through her system?

"Chocolate is tricky to work with," she babbled. "It's better to do favors like these at night when it's cooler."

And when the bakery was empty.

"A lot of things are better made at night," he murmured.

He was flirting with her.

Vivian wondered if it was bad form to do a butt-wiggling victory dance in the alley this late while surrounded by chocolate lingerie.

"You're melting."

"What?"

How'd he know? Before she could figure it out, Zane angled the hand he captured up so the streetlight shone on it. Her heart pounding at the feel of his fingers on hers, Vivian caught a glance of the streak of chocolate.

"Um, yeah. It's warm," she started to say.

Then he shifted her hand to his lips.

And sucked on her finger.

"Delicious."

Desire, hot and needy, coiled tight in her belly, making Vivian want to moan.

"Oh. My. God."

She didn't know she'd spoke the chant out loud until a wicked smile flashed over Zane's face. Not sure if she should be embarrassed or grateful for the invitation in that smile, Vivian reluctantly pulled her fingers away from those tempting lips.

"Do you live nearby?"

Oh, yeah.

Her arm was in the air, ready to point toward the stairs

that led to her apartment over the bakery. Inside her apartment was a bed. A big, comfy, private bed.

But something made her freeze midgesture.

Dozens of stories ran through her head. Stories about Zane Bennett and his legendary skill with women. The only thing more legendary was his inability to refuse a challenge.

Ding.

Vivian lowered her hand, letting it rest on his shoulder, her fingers tracing little circles on the back of his neck to buy time as her mind raced.

She took a step closer, so their bodies nearly brushed, but not quite. Then she gave him her sexiest smile. She sighed, deep, so her breasts skimmed over his chest. And watched his eyes blur.

Good, she thought as she stepped back enough to let him miss the contact. She had his attention.

"I have some damage control to do here," she said, lifting the box of ruined chocolates and giving it a shake. "Why don't we meet somewhere tomorrow?"

"Somewhere?" he repeated, his eyes boring into hers as if he could see all the way to the depths of her soul where her secrets were hidden. "Where did you have in mind?"

Oh, so many possibilities came to mind.

A hotel. A motel. Hot Tub Heaven. A mattress store. The back room of the bakery, where there was an ample supply of chocolate to pour over his body, then lick off.

"Drinks," she said, shoving the words out fast before any of those other ideas could escape. "We could get a drink."

"A drink sounds good." She had to give him credit. He didn't look upset about being put off. "Does Carvellos still have great appetizers?"

She'd figured on meeting at the pub, with her thoughts

on easy access to her apartment. Vivian's breath caught, delight pouring through her. With its moody lighting, private booths and piano bar, Carvellos was the go-to spot for romantic dates.

And he wanted to take her there.

Oh, my.

"They still have an amazing appetizer menu," she said, blaming the giddiness in her voice on the fact that he wanted to romance her. Romance. Her. That was worthy of another "oh, my."

Vivian bit her lip, her gaze shifting toward the stairs and her apartment. *No*, she scolded herself. *Stick with the plan.* She wanted his attention for more than one night. Now she had it, along with an invitation for drinks at the swankiest spot in town. "Is six okay?"

"Perfect." His smile was like a magnet, pulling her closer. Vivian didn't object when he reached out to slide one hand over her hair, his fingers tangling in the strands as he cupped the back of her neck.

Staring into her eyes with that hypnotic gaze of his, Zane slowly lowered his head until his mouth was a breath away from hers. Vivian was sure her heart stopped. She was pretty sure the world stopped. She tried to tell herself to keep her expectations somewhere in the realm of realistic. Just because she'd spent years dreaming about Zane's kissing prowess didn't mean it'd be like she'd imagined.

Then his lips slid over hers.

A soft, gentle glide just a hint stronger than a whisper.

Her breath released in a slow shudder as she sank into the sweetness of it. Almost as sweet as her Bavarian cream. She started to relax, some of that tense anticipation drifting away as he shifted angles. Just the tiniest shift.

His tongue caressed her bottom lip. So, so sweet.

Then he nipped, a scrape of teeth over the full softness

of her mouth. Desire shot, sharp and hot, through Vivian's belly, sparking a desperate need.

She gasped.

His tongue plunged.

It swept over hers, coiled and danced. Vivian melted. She straight-up melted into a puddle of desire as he took the kiss from hot to incendiary with his magic tongue. She might have kissed him back; she wasn't sure. Everything became a tangled blur of desire, edgy need pounding through her body, settling deep in her belly. Her breasts swelled, nipples beaded with passion.

Vivian had never felt so much.

The kiss might have lasted a minute. It might have lasted forever. All she knew was that she didn't want it to end.

But apparently Zane didn't hear that silent plea, because he pulled away. Slowly, he eased back. One last press of his lips against hers and he lifted his head.

Feeling as if her lashes weighed a ton, Vivian had to force her eyelids open. It took longer to swallow the knot blocking her airway and breathe.

Zane's expression was intense. He stared for a long moment, first into her eyes, making her want to squirm. Then his gaze shifted to her mouth. His eyes darkened; his head shifted just a little. Vivian held her breath, wondering if he'd kiss her again. Then his eyes met hers again.

"I'll see you tomorrow," he said, his hand releasing her neck, leaving her feeling cold without the pressure. He stepped back, watching.

Waiting.

For what? she wondered. Until he realized he was being a gentleman. He was waiting for her to go wherever she was going, to make sure she was safe.

She couldn't go upstairs to her apartment. Mike might

have mentioned that his little sister lived above the bakery. Besides, knowing he realized where she lived might be too much temptation. What if he walked her to her door? There was no way she'd be able to resist yanking him inside with her.

So she dug her keys out of her pocket and unlocked the bakery door. Nothing to resist here, since no amount of sizzle could inspire her to do him in the same place that Mrs. Enid indulged in her daily cruller. A girl had to have some standards, after all.

As she pushed the door open, Vivian looked over her shoulder. Zane stood at the edge of the sidewalk, both hands in his pockets as he rocked back on the heels of his motorcycle boots. He wore a hint of a smile on his face and his eyes were hot with appreciation as he stared at her butt. Finally, his grin widening, he met her eyes.

"Tomorrow," he said again, giving her a jaunty salute by tapping two fingers to his brow.

"Tomorrow," she echoed, hesitating before she stepped through the door. He waited, she noticed, until she'd turned the lock behind her before he headed for the alley. He must be staying with Lenny, Vivian realized with a groan. She had to force herself not to chase after him.

As soon as he was out of sight, she dropped into one of the padded ice cream chairs, letting her box of ruined chocolates fall onto the table with a thunk—quickly followed by her head.

What had she done?

She'd had a chance to have hot, wild, rock-the-walls-and-make-the-roof-shake sex with Zane Bennett.

Something she'd been dreaming about since she was seventeen. She'd heard plenty of stories. Oh, not like Mike came home boasting about the Bennett brothers' sexual exploits. But there'd been plenty of things she'd overheard him and his little circle of friends say, usually in tones of awe. And the women in town were more than vocal in singing their odes of delight to the wonder that was Zane's sexual talents. They probably sang about Xander, too, but Vivian's focus had always been on Zane.

So she knew that he was a man who loved a challenge. One who thrived on a dare. Which gave her an easy option if he balked at getting naked. The only downside to the dare option was as soon as he stepped up to the challenge, he was done.

She'd seen it plenty of times.

Guys loved the chase. But the minute they scored, they were off to the next challenge.

But Vivian wasn't sure she wanted to settle for only one single round with Zane. Oh, she wasn't thinking she wanted forever—who could make that kind of decision before sex and a playlist comparison? But she knew she wanted more than one time.

And the only way she'd get more than one was to keep Zane interested.

Intrigued.

Challenged.

Vivian gave the box of chocolates a little shake as she headed for the kitchen.

Oh, yeah. This was going to be fun.

5

ZANE ROLLED OUT of bed—or in this case, off Lenny's couch—with one thing in mind.

The same thing that'd been on his mind all night.

The sexy blonde with the mile-long legs and chocolate lingerie.

Delicious.

He wouldn't mind tasting more.

More than just that nibble of her finger, and definitely more of that chocolate. She'd sparked a hunger in him that he didn't remember feeling before. One he had to explore. If only to see if that combination of laughter and lust had been a fluke. Laughter, lust and a gorgeous blonde? A perfect combination.

Who said chivalry was dead?

Zane knew it was alive because he'd used up his share for a lifetime. He'd used it walking away from the sexy blonde instead of talking his way into her bed.

Oh, he'd had the lines all—well, lined up. A little charm, another taste of that chocolate and a suggestion that they head to her place, where he might get to peek under that silky blouse of hers to see if the lingerie she wore was as sexy as the kind she made.

But first, he should find out her name.

How else was he going to call it out when he came?

A quick check of his watch assured him that he had an hour and a half before he had to meet the family for breakfast, then later to hit the high school to register for the reunion. Plenty of time to do a little recon on the blonde, take a pass at Quinn and hit the florist for a bouquet to take his mother.

Given all the women he had to charm, Zane took the time to cram himself into Lenny's minuscule excuse for a shower. Damned thing was almost as small as the ones on the subs he'd served on. Not nearly as clean, though.

He was halfway down the outside stairs when he realized that, hey, he wasn't bored anymore.

Which was probably why his grin was so wide when he strode through the wide glass doors of the bakery. It smelled amazing. Yeasty breads, sugary treats and hot fruit wafted through the air in tempting invitation.

He noted that, like the new blue-and-white-striped awning, the interior decor had been upgraded. There were a half-dozen small round tables, apparently for people who couldn't wait to get out the door to dive into their baked goods.

"Can I help you?" The offer came from the pretty woman behind the counter, blond curls waving around a Kewpie doll face.

"I'm looking for…" Shit. Zane frowned. He really did need her name. "The baker."

"Oh? Did you want to place a special order?"

"Sure."

She gave him a narrow-eyed look, one that said she obviously knew who he was. But after a long moment, she stepped away from the counter to call through a set of swinging doors.

"Customer to see you."

And there it was.

The sexy siren's voice called out from the kitchen. He couldn't make out her words, but that husky timbre was enough to ease a tension in his gut he hadn't even realized he was holding.

Lips pursed, the Kewpie doll returned to the counter and gave him that look again.

"She'll be out in a few minutes. She's on the phone." As if realizing that didn't sound exactly professional, she added, "She's talking with one of the owners and can't be interrupted."

Remembering Mike mentioning that his parents were traveling, Zane realized they must be running things long-distance. He wondered if they knew their sexy baker made naughty candies in her spare time.

A quick scan of the display counter assured him that while varied, pretty and delicious in appearance, there was nothing suggestive on those glass shelves.

He wasn't surprised. Mr. and Mrs. Harris were nice enough people, but they leaned toward the stuffy side. The kind who would be horrified to even realize that chocolate could be molded into sexy undies, let alone that it was being done in their own bakery. He remembered their reaction to catching Mike with a *Playboy*—threats of a monastery, running his brain through a carwash or, as they'd settled on, grounding the guy for two months of hard labor.

"Did you want to buy something while you wait?" the girl asked halfheartedly. If her expression was anything to go by, she was sure the answer would be no.

So Zane was determined to say yes.

A quick glance at the cupcake-shaped clock on the wall reminded him that he had two more tasks and thirty minutes before he had to leave to meet his brother. But he'd bet his mom would be just as happy with a baked treat as she would flowers. With one task knocked off his list, he could use that time to spend with his own personal treat.

With that in mind, he glanced toward the glistening display case.

"How about a cupcake?" he requested, pointing to a pretty yellow one mounded high with swirls of whipped cream and topped with a glossy strawberry. It looked like the kind of thing Quinn would enjoy.

Deciding the sultry blonde was more the sexy devil's food cake type, he pointed to another, this one looking as if it'd been dipped in chocolate that'd hardened beneath the swirls of lighter chocolate frosting and decorated with chocolate curls.

"Which one did you want?" the kewpie doll asked.

"I'll take both." Literally and figuratively. "And box up a half dozen of those there, the ones with the roses."

After paying, he grabbed the chocolate cupcake and headed behind the counter, leaving the box and strawberry confection next to the register to grab on his way out.

"Wait," the Kewpie doll stammered, trying to move fast enough to block his way. "You can't go back there."

"Sure I can. Mrs. Harris used to let me do it all the time. Mike'll vouch for me," he assured her.

She looked like she didn't know if she should argue or not. Before she could decide, a pair of women entered the bakery with a jingle of the bell over the door.

Zane used the distraction to slip around her and into the back room. Letting the door swing shut behind him to close off the storefront from the kitchen, his gaze skipped over the stacked trays of bread in various tempting varieties and what looked like a wall of cookies, muffins and a rainbow of cupcakes waiting for frosting.

Overhead lights glinted on the stainless-steel tables in the center of the room, two set with baking equipment while the third held a five-tier cake currently naked but for the little sticks propped between the layers.

A sugar fiend's paradise, he decided. Then his gaze found true paradise in the far corner. Her back to him, Zane enjoyed the unobstructed view of one of the sweetest butts he'd ever seen encased in a flirty skirt that cupped said butt, hugged slender hips and held tight to long legs all the way to just below the knee. As she shifted from one foot to the other, a series of tiny pleats played peek-a-boo with the back of her knees.

Who knew knees could be sexy?

He listened to what sounded like a report on a week's worth of baking with half an ear as he settled one hip on a stainless-steel table and waited for her to notice him.

Eighteen seconds.

It took her just over a quarter of a minute to turn around. She made a little choking sound, gulping down the last of her sentence before giving him a little finger wave.

Zane waved back with the cupcake, liking the way her eyes lit up as she smiled.

"Um, I really should get to decorating now," she said into the phone, her eyes tracking Zane's moves as plucked off a chocolate curl and popped it into his mouth. "I've got that wedding cake to finish by two."

She rolled her eyes, giving the won't-shut-up hand signal.

Impressed with what he'd tasted so far, Zane broke off a chunk of the chocolate shell and licked the sweet frosting from the edge.

"Delicious," he murmured before offering her the piece. When she shook her head, he popped it into his mouth.

Damned delicious. He licked a smudge of frosting off his thumb. When her eyes blurred, he did it again.

By the time she hung up the phone, they were both pretty obviously turned on.

"You think you can seduce me with chocolate?"

Points to her for being quick on the uptake.

"As a matter of fact." Zane swept his finger over the side of the cupcake's frosting, scooping up a dab of chocolate. His eyes locked on Vivian's, he licked it off, grinning when her pupils dilated.

"I thought we were meeting at six," she said breathlessly, her eyes shifting from him to the door that led to the bakery, then back again.

He grinned, not sure why it amused him to make her so nervous.

"I wanted to stop in for cupcakes," he explained. "And from what I'm tasting, yours are definitely delicious."

"If you think my chocolate cupcake is amazing, you should taste my vanilla cream," she teased, her smile widening into a teasing grin.

A niggling reminder tapped again, telling himself he knew her from somewhere.

"Are you attending the reunion?" he asked, knowing he'd never get another taste of frosting if he admitted that he knew her from somewhere but couldn't remember where.

"Nope, no reunion for me. But I'll try to catch a few of the events."

Events?

"What events?"

She tilted her head to look behind him at the clock and gave a wide grimace before he could puzzle it out.

"It totally bums me out to say this, but I have to get to

work," she told him, pulling out a sexy little pout that made him want to lick that bottom lip.

"I should get going, too." After all, he had to see his mom, meet the guys, win a challenge. "You probably have some cupcakes to bake."

"Actually—" she wet her lips "—I'm playing with frosting today."

Hot damn.

She dipped her finger into the bowl, drawing out a scoop of fluffy white frosting and holding it high.

Zane tore his eyes off her face long enough to glance at it, then had to look again.

"Is that glittering?"

"Mmm, edible glitter in the frosting. I think it adds a little something special." Her eyes not leaving his, she swept her tongue over her finger, licking off half the frosting and sending a shaft of heat through Zane's body so hard and fast that his jeans almost ripped.

"Want to taste?"

Instead of letting him lick her finger, though, she gave him her mouth. Soft, wet and tempting, her lips teased, her teeth scraped. The kiss went from playful to incendiary in a sweep of her tongue.

Then, way too soon, she pulled away, leaving behind the tempting flavor of vanilla and a little something special.

"Was that to hold me until drinks?" he asked, his hands rubbing circles over the soft fabric covering her hips.

"It's just something to keep in mind. You know, in case you meet anyone or hear anything that makes you tempted to skip out on our date."

"What I might hear?" He grinned. "You have a rep I should know about?"

"You're one to talk about reps." Vivian laughed, the

sound both sexy and sweet at the same time. "It'd take me a lifetime to even work up to a tenth of your reputation, Mr. Bad Boy Bennett."

"Good point. So what am I going to hear?"

Her gaze narrowed, those big brown eyes intense as she studied his face. But instead of answering, she shook her head.

"Just keep that kiss in mind," she suggested.

As if there was any chance he'd forget.

"What're you doing later?" he asked, keeping his voice low. No point in making it easy for the Kewpie doll to stir up gossip.

"Later, when?"

"Later, after we meet for drinks."

A smile curved those full lips. It was a tempting sort of a smile that sent a hot shot of desire straight though his body. God, he couldn't remember ever flashing so hot, so fast, for a woman before.

"I have some chocolate to replace," she said, running her tongue over her bottom lip, then lifting one arched brow. "You remember the chocolate from last night?"

"In vivid detail, as a matter of fact. I even dreamed about a few of those chocolates."

"Actually—" she leaned in closer so her words were a breath of air over his skin "—a few of those chocolate designs were based on my very own lingerie."

He thought of the various odes to sexy underthings he'd seen the night before. *Oh, yeah.* Even hotter.

"How about I help you with that? Since it's my fault your other batch was ruined." This might be the first time he'd ever used chocolate as a ploy to get a woman naked.

"Are you any good?"

"Babe, you have no idea." Zane's smile turned wicked. "I promise you won't be disappointed."

"I guess we'll see."

Zane wanted to show her here and now just how satisfied she'd be, but he could hear the clock ticking behind him.

"Tonight," he promised, heading for the exit with the chocolate cupcake in hand. *Oh, yeah.* One hand on the door, he glanced back. "Just one question."

She hitched herself onto the desk, one leg crossed over the other so her skirt fluttered at her thighs as she swung her foot.

"Only one?"

His eyes locked on those legs, Zane wondered if he could actually feel his brain cells dying from lust overload.

"Just one." He pulled his gaze up to her face, appreciating the sassy smile playing over those vivid red lips. "What's your name?"

Her laugh filled the room as sweetly as the sugar already scenting the air.

"Vivian."

Zane knew he'd never slept with a Vivian before, but he did a quick memory check anyway. Because there was something so damned familiar about her.

"Nice to meet you, Vivian."

"The pleasure is all mine, Zane." The words were a husky purr that suited silk sheets and candlelight.

His grin flashed.

"Believe me, it will be."

He'd make sure of it.

"Oh, Zane?"

He looked over his shoulder.

"One more thing." She swiped up another scoop of frosting, then delicately licked the glittery white confection off her finger. His blood zoomed south so fast, Zane was surprised he didn't black out. He grabbed hold of the door frame, just in case.

"Anything," he said. "Especially if it includes frosting."

"It might." Vivian smiled, one foot swinging to and fro, each pass making her skirt flutter and showing that sexy hint of thigh. "Of course, you have to show up to find out. With that in mind—" she put her finger in her mouth again, sucking the frosting clean off, and Zane had to remind himself to breathe "—I dare you to show up this evening—no matter what you might hear about me."

"What?" He shook his head to clear the lust fog. "Why?"

"Oh, I have my reasons," she promised. "If you take the dare, you'll find out what they are."

"I never say no to a dare." Zane aimed a finger her way. "You're on."

"I can't wait." With that, Vivian dipped her spatula into the stainless-steel bowl, spread a thick layer of white glitter over the first tier of cake, then looked up with a flutter of her lashes. "Maybe later you'll be saying that again."

YOU'RE ON.

Those words played out in Zane's head like a soundtrack to a very enticing reel of images. What did she have in mind? Oh, he'd clued in to the sexual innuendo just fine.

"Hi."

But there was more going on.

"Zane?

He might serve in EOD instead of Intelligence, but he was trained well enough in cryptology to recognize a hidden message when he heard it. Now he just had to decipher the meaning.

"Have you slipped into a coma? Or did you forget why you knocked on my door?"

Zane blinked the pretty brunette into focus. From the expression on her face, she wasn't used to being ignored.

With good reason. There was nothing ignorable about Quinn Oswald.

With that in mind, Zane focused on the matter at hand. Winning the challenge.

"Hello, Quinn." He dug down for his most charming smile. "I brought you a cupcake."

6

ZANE COULDN'T STOP thinking about Vivian.

She'd stayed front and center in his mind during his chat over coffee and a cupcake with Quinn. She'd lurked in the background during his visit with his mom—which was pretty damned polite, since the thoughts he was having were totally unsuited to have around mothers. And here she was, still filling his head as he headed for the reunion registration.

He'd never obsessed over a woman before. Why would he when there were so many more out there to get to know? But there was something about Vivian that intrigued the hell out of him.

Could be the siren's smile of hers, with those full inviting lips and hint of an overbite? Or the invitation in her sloe eyes? Or the body? Oh, yeah, that body was worth a few million obsessive thoughts. But as gorgeous as the package was, his head was filled just as often with the memory of her laughter, the way her eyes lit up. Her clever quips and the comfortable ease she seemed to have with the sexier side of life. And then there was the frosting.

He parked his Harley in the visitors' lot of the high

school and sat there for a moment, paying tribute to that frosting.

Or maybe it was her dare. What was up with that? He puzzled over that as he strode across the high school court-yard, following the hand-lettered signs to the auditorium.

"Yo, Bennett."

Zane lifted a hand to return the greeting, but didn't slow his stride.

"Hi, Zane."

The petite redhead required a quick flip through his mental files.

"Hey, Stacey." Reluctantly slowing his pace, he waited for the vivacious former cheerleader captain to join him. "How's it going?"

In their three-minute chat, she managed to touch his cheek, his ear, his shoulder, arm and chest. Time to say goodbye, he decided when her fingers drifted south.

"Better go," he excused, tilting his head toward the re-union signs. "I've got to get registered, find my brother, that kind of thing."

"Give me a call while you're here." She leaned into him, her breasts echoing the invitation. "We can do a little remi-niscing of our own."

With a smile and a noncommittal grunt, he disentangled himself and continued toward the auditorium. Invites like that weren't rare on these visits home. But his lack of in-terest was.

He wasn't interested in a quickie, just a good time or a fast, pants-around-the-ankles ride down memory lane.

Zane's feet stopped so fast, he almost face planted it into the side of the building.

What the hell was going on?

Sure, he wanted to see Vivian again. Yeah, to his recollection she was the hottest woman he'd ever met. And yeah, the sexual explosion potential was intense.

But that was no reason to obsess.

Not to the point of losing interest in other women.

That was just crazy.

He had to get Vivian out of his head.

He had to keep this on the down low.

At least until he'd figured out what she was up to, and what was going on between them. And, yeah, most likely after that, too.

Because if there was one thing his buddies were, it was a pain in the ass when it came to trying to ferret out information and use it.

Zane put his game face on. Anything less would be fodder for the idiot brigade. And while most of the hometown gang were pretty lame at digging up deets, Xander was the king.

Zane stopped inside the doors, rocked back on his heels and looked around.

Huh.

Talk about distractions.

Maybe those sayings about time were true. The place did look smaller than it had back in school. Probably because the three dozen people milling around were adults instead of teens. Or it could be the big-ass float in the middle of the basketball court shaped like a panther wearing a sailor cap.

"What the hell is that?" he asked when he'd made his way around the float to where his friends were gathered.

"Reunion float," Lenny said, his tone pure *duh*. "For the parade."

"Parade?" Zane exchanged appalled looks with his brother. "Seriously?"

"Seriously." Mike nodded. "We're honoring you guys, remember?"

"With a stuffed cat?" Xander choked out.

"What's a parade without a float?"

"A…"

"Parade?" Zane finished in the same tone he'd use if Mike said they'd be straddling IEDs down Main Street.

"Yep. Most of the members of the marching band are back for the reunion and five of the eight baton twirlers." Mike continued his parade playbook, listing names of their graduating class who'd be revisiting their former glory. Zane stopped listening after the cheerleaders.

"Seriously…" Zane dropped into the chair next to his brother and shook his head.

"I say we sneak back in here tonight," Xander said, leaning toward Zane, his voice low. "Dismantle the cat and burn that freaking hat."

"There's still time to mount a strategic retreat."

"You're forgetting one thing."

Their eyes met. Zane sighed.

At the same time, they said, "Mom."

Ever since they got home, she'd been beaming.

She'd beamed her way through a big family dinner the night before when she'd told them that her entire book club had started reading Navy SEAL romances to celebrate her sweet boys being honored as heroes.

She'd beamed while their sister Kerri's kids had peppered them with a million questions about the military, and hadn't even dimmed when they'd begged for blood and gore.

She'd beamed her way through the cupcakes Zane had brought her earlier that day while talking to the reporter who'd called to ask what it was like to raise two heroes.

And she'd beamed her way through the four phone calls

that'd come in while he was there, each one checking to see if she needed a ride, an extra photographer or, hey, how about a videographer for the big event.

"Fine," Zane muttered. "But I'm not riding on that panther."

No way. No how. He shook his head. If he was going to ride anything, it was going to be the sexy blonde. Zane couldn't recall a woman ever sticking in his head like Vivian was, but considering the nature of the thoughts, he couldn't say he was sorry. He just wished he knew what the hell she meant with that dare.

"Something's up with you," Xander said, his narrow gaze searching. "What is it?"

Zane debated telling his brother about the sexy blonde with the erotic chocolate and creative cupcakes. He'd probably know why Vivian was so familiar. Xander knew damn near everything.

Before Zane could mention her, though, the rest of the guys arrived with a clatter of metal chairs, raucous laughter and loud greetings.

"Xander!" Zane caught the loud squeal just before he caught the curvy brunette issuing it. She landed on his lap, latched her very enthusiastic mouth on his and attempted a friendly tonsillectomy before he could pull away.

"Welcome home," she purred, her fingers slinking their way down his chest.

Feeling like he was wrestling with a very curvy octopus, Zane disentangled himself from the woman, setting her aside with a smile.

"Nice to see you, too, Tiffany. But I'm Zane, not Xander." He grinned when the brunette gave a loud "Oops," then slithered over to offer the same greeting to his brother. Xander looked anything but thrilled.

"It's not fair," Lenny complained when she'd been sent on her way. "The two of you always got all the girls."

"Not all the girls," Xander muttered.

"Speaking of girls," Kyle said, slapping a hand on both brothers' shoulders. "Either of you made any progress with Quinn yet?"

For the briefest second, Zane thought he saw something in his brother's eyes. Xander didn't say anything, though, so Zane jumped in with, "It's only been one day."

"Since when has time been an issue?" Kyle wondered.

"You giving up?" Mike challenged.

"Right." Zane grinned. "Like that's going to happen. I saw Quinn earlier. Took her a cupcake, even."

"A cupcake?" Kyle laughed. "Is she eight?"

"Fancy cupcake topped with swirls of whipped cream and one large glossy strawberry." Zane looked around, gauging their expressions before adding, "And sprinkles. The glittery ones."

"Whoa," Kyle breathed with the same rapt expression he wore when he heard one of the brothers' military stories. Impressed, fascinated and a little awestruck. "Glittery sprinkles?"

"You, my friend, are the man." Lenny slapped him on the back.

"We should have put money on this one. It's definitely going to get interesting," Mike said with a regretful laugh.

That was when it hit him.

He stared at Mike's smile and the slightly crooked twist of his lips that signified the guy thought he had the upper hand.

Shit.

Vivian was Mike's sister. His little sister. Dating her could very well be a violation of the bro code.

Couldn't it?

Zane couldn't remember Mike ever voicing an objection to the thought of a friend dating his sister. Just the previous night he'd even laughed at the idea of Lenny hitting on her. But he'd issued no dire warnings or concern. Was that just because Lenny was a class-A dweeb? Or did Mike apply the idea that Vivian could take care of herself to any guy?

Suddenly the dare made perfect sense.

She'd figured he'd make the connection. She was obviously aware of the bro code. And she clearly knew him well enough to figure out the right button to push to ensure she got what she wanted.

Zane leaned back and smiled.

Damned if that didn't make her even sexier.

OH, BOY.

At five fifty, Vivian parked her car up the street from Carvellos and flipped down the visor to check her appearance. She puffed out a nervous breath, then slicked an extra coating of Carnal Crimson, dabbing a hint of gloss on the cushioned fullness of her bottom lip to give it a sexy pout. Skimming one Glistening Midnight nail under her bottom lashes, she gave an extra hint of smudge to her liner before shaking her head so her hair fell in a silken wing over her left eye.

There. Ready for drinks and a little something extra, she decided as she slipped out of the car. She dropped her keys into her tiny black patent leather cylinder purse, tucking the chain over her shoulder as she took another long breath and, hips swaying thanks to her four-inch retro peep-toe heels, made her way down the sidewalk toward the restaurant.

As she passed the floral boutique, she checked her appearance again in the wall of windows. Her sleeveless red-and-white polka-dotted blouse had a sweetheart neckline she'd accented with an oversized beaded necklace. She'd tucked the silk into a high-waisted sailor-button pencil skirt that hit just above the knee. The look was pure vintage, sexy with class, she concluded, tugging the fabric at her hips a little to smooth out a crease.

Not only did the forties look suit her, hopefully it was different enough to keep Zane's attention and keep him distracted enough to forget her last name. And, more important, who her brother was.

She sashayed with deceptive ease to the door of Carvellos, not breaking her stride except to nod her thanks to the older gentleman who held open the door. She could feel his eyes on her butt and considered it a good sign. She needed all the confidence she could get to continue into the bar.

Not because she was afraid of her date with Zane.

But because she was afraid it wouldn't happen.

She knew the odds of Zane not realizing who she was— or more specifically, realizing who's sister she was—were dancing somewhere between slim and none.

Oh, she was pretty sure he'd show.

She'd dared him.

But that didn't mean he'd show alone. He could bring Mike. He could stay just long enough to explain why he wasn't going to stay.

She took a deep, cleansing breath and told herself to channel Lola. What would Lola say? To think positive. The only way to live the dream was to believe the dream. To put it all out there and make it happen.

Vivian wiggled into the most romantic corner booth she could wheedle and ordered a sparkling water. No point enjoying wine until she knew she'd enjoy the evening, too.

She pulled out her cell phone. No cancellation message. That was a good sign, wasn't it?

Half the time, Vivian felt like her dreams were a tease.

All too often she got within kissing distance of her goal and, poof, there it went. No big payoff, no awesome climax, nothing.

Because, why? Because she always blew it.

She shouldn't have told him her name.

She should have teased instead, said she'd tell him tonight.

Maybe she shouldn't have let him in on what she made at The Sweet Spot, either. Sure, a lot of guys saw that as a turn-on, but there were just as many who subscribed to the prude theory. Like her brother.

And he was Mike's friend.

Then again, so was Lenny.

Before she'd finished her confused sigh, Zanc walkcd in. And all of her doubts took a backseat to the sight of how gorgeous the man was. Vivian sat up a little straighter. Shoulders back, chin high and chest probably jiggling because her heart was beating so fast, she smiled and sent him a little wave.

"Vivian," he greeted as he joined her.

"Zane."

"So you're Mike's little sister, hmm?"

"Aah, so the dare worked." Vivian smiled. "How many times did you consider bailing?"

"Bailing? I'll have you know I'm trained to confront conflicts of all shapes and sizes. I fearlessly face down explosives, disarm bombs and disable volatile chemicals. Sometimes all three before breakfast."

"Tell me more." Delighted, Vivian put on a wide-eyed look of fascination, even adding a little eyelash flutter for good measure.

"I train with the best. I'm one of the elite. There's no challenge devised that I won't face." He leaned in, his smile almost hypnotic as he teased. "Baby, I never bail."

"I can't tell you how glad I am to hear that," Vivian declared as the waiter brought Zane a beer and refilled her water.

"But here's the thing—" he started to say as soon as the waiter left.

"No," she moaned. "Not the thing."

There was only one thing of Zane's that she wanted to hear about.

"Here's the thing," Zane continued, laughing. "Some guys have rules about buddies dating their sisters. Sisters, cousins, moms. Guys get weird thinking the women in their lives have sex. They get even weirder when they know the guy putting the moves on that sex."

Lips pursed, Vivian propped her elbow on the table and rested her chin on her fist.

"Aren't you taking a leap there, assuming we'd definitely be having sex?"

Zane blinked, looked horrified for one second, then shook his head.

"I'm speaking generally, not specifically." He narrowed his eyes. "Are you saying that you see this thing between us as platonic?"

"Of course not. I plan on having a great deal of sex with you," she purred. "A mind-blowing amount, as a matter of fact."

"Mind-blowing, hmm?"

"Indeed." She reached out with her free hand to trail her fingers over his knee. Up his thigh, then back down again. Oh, baby, even through denim, his muscles were rigidly impressive.

He clamped his hand down, locking hers down on his thigh.

"Only one thing."

"Only one?"

"Only one." Zane entwined his fingers through hers. "Your brother."

"Oh, please," she objected. "Like you're afraid of my brother? The man wears argyle socks and loafers, for crying out loud."

Zane's snicker escaped before he could stop it, then he shook his head. "Mike's footwear isn't the issue. The fact that you're his little sister is the issue."

Vivian debated a handful of approaches.

She could keep blathering about her brother. That'd put an end to either of their interest in anything after a while. Mike was like a sedative.

She could offer him an easy out, a simple excuse to end the evening so he wasn't in danger of violating his bro code. Given there was a lifelong friendship involved, that'd be the nicest thing to do.

She could seduce Zane into forgetting about the bro code, which would ensure her one night of dreams-come-true ecstasy.

Or she could do the unthinkable.

Vivian took a deep breath, her eyes locked on Zane's face. He had such a sweet smile and sexy eyes. And there were dreams at stake here, dammit.

So she reached into her bag to do the unthinkable.

"What are you doing?"

She finished tapping out her brother's number.

"Getting you bro-code clearance."

"Mike," she said the minute he picked up. "Let's play what-if. What if I have the hots for one of your friends? What if this friend wants to make a move but he's worried about upsetting you, so I want to make the move instead? What would your feelings be on that?"

"He's afraid of me?" Mike laughed. "Wish him luck."

"Okeydokey," she agreed, ending the call and giving Zane her most seductive smile.

Zane gave her a long look, the kind that made her want to squirm in her seat and breathe a little heavier.

Then he smiled.

"You know he thinks you're referring to Lenny, don't you?"

Vivian ran her tongue over her lower lip and leaned into the table. Just enough to highlight her cleavage. She waited until Zane's gaze returned to her eyes before giving a delicate little shrug.

"Can I help it if my brother is an idiot?"

7

Zane didn't remember a lot of details about the drive back to the bakery. He remembered even less about the journey up the back stairs, except that the view of Vivian's ass swaying ahead of him was enough to make his mouth water.

"You do amazing things to a skirt," he murmured.

And for a sexy look, he realized as Vivian reached the landing and gave him a smoldering over-the-shoulder look that damn near set his shorts on fire.

"You should see what I do for lingerie."

Damn.

"I'm looking forward to that."

Oh, boy, was he ever. Figuring, why resist temptation when it was right there in his face, he cupped the sweet curve of her butt while she unlocked the door. Firm and full, and purely awesome.

The minute Vivian twisted the doorknob, Zane angled himself behind her, pressing against that deliciously tight ass. God, he wanted her.

He pressed his palm against the door and shoved.

Before she finished laughing, he had her inside, her back against the now closed door and his body up against hers.

One hand still cupping her ass, the other dived into her hair, cradling the back of her neck as he took her mouth in huge, intense bites. Tongue, teeth, lips melded, danced, explored.

She tasted amazing.

And he was starving.

Ready to feast, Zane pulled her hips against his and groaned. Great fit. He fisted her skirt in his hand, more than ready to find out if she was a perfect fit.

"Wait," she gasped.

What? No.

Zane clenched his teeth and, with a deep breath, froze.

Figuring it was the only way, he lifted both hands high and stepped back. He was a man who thrived on challenges, but, damn, all of the challenges he was facing on the road to getting Vivian naked was going to push him to his limits.

But the lady said wait. So, forcing his heart rate to slow, he waited.

Without taking her eyes off his, she slid out from between him and the door. That mysterious smile that had hooked him so hard played over her red lips, the rest of her features shrouded in the dim light.

"I was thinking of you when I picked this skirt," she told him. "It's sailor-style."

"Sailor-style?"

"Mmm, see these buttons?" She waved one hand toward her hip, game show–hostess style. Zane's mouth dried up imagining the prize he was about to win. "They lead to doing it sailor-style."

"Guess it's a good thing that I'm an experienced sailor."

"Indeed. And after we do it sailor-style, we can try cupcake-style." She dabbed the tip of her tongue to the center of her top lip. "I have frosting waiting. With glitter."

Zane wasn't sure if she said something after that because of the sudden buzzing in his ears.

She flipped open the first button at her waist.

His mouth went dry.

She flipped the opposite button.

The blood whooshed right out of his head. Zane leaned back against the door, just in case.

One by one, she released the buttons. She gave the tiniest of shimmies and the skirt fell right off those hips and hit the floor. Leaving her standing there in sexy red high heels, that pretty blouse that cupped her breasts and fluttered at her hips, showing off her stockings. Sexy nude ones with lace at the thighs.

Zane could barely think over the roaring in his head.

While he was reeling from the sight of stockings—damn, baby, stockings!—she bent at the waist. Elongating that gorgeous length of creamy, stocking-clad thigh and thrusting her butt in the air to give him a peek of black satin edged in red.

Holy crap, she was wearing black-and-red panties.

Zane could resist a lot of things, but not black-and-red panties. No way, no how.

It took all his willpower to rip his gaze off that temptation and look back at her face. A long swath of blond hair swept over her face, partially obscuring one eye in that femme fatale style she rocked so well.

It wasn't until he felt her fingers close over his that he realized she'd pressed something into his hand.

Frowning, he glanced down.

"What…" He clenched the fabric in his fist. "Why?"

"You said you liked my skirt."

Oh, yeah, he did.

"I like that blouse, too."

"Do you, now?"

She skimmed her hand up her waist, her fingers dancing over the shiny polka-dotted fabric. She cupped her breasts just long enough to make him groan, then slid her fingers up behind her neck. The straps drooped, but didn't drop to reveal her breasts. It took all of Zane's control to resist shoving them down the rest of the way.

She did something with the fabric at her side, and bless that blouse, it dropped for him.

Leaving her standing there in those stockings, a tiny triangle of red-trimmed black silk and glorious skin. Miles and miles of skin.

His eyes latched on to her breasts. He barely resisted the temptation to check to see if his jaw dropped. Because those were definitely jaw-dropping breasts.

Full and firm, tipped with perfect berry-shaped nipples.

"Wow," he said when he finally met her gaze again. "Just, wow."

"Oops, sorry." Her laugh was a soft husky breath. "I guess I forgot the lingerie."

"What, no lingerie? We'll have to try it again. Later," he murmured, cupping her breasts reverently in both hands. Much later.

"Should we take this into the other room?" Vivian suggested, her fingers tiptoeing their way down his chest to his belly before drawing teasing little circles just above his belt buckle.

The other room sounded good. Hell, the floor sounded good.

Still Zane shook his head.

"Not yet."3

SO THIS WAS HEAVEN.

Vivian considered herself a woman well-schooled in the sexual arts. She'd memorized *The Joy of Sex*, the *Kama*

Sutra and the *One Hundred Sexual Positions* coloring book. She'd watched *Fifty Shades of Grey* twice, *Magic Mike* and the sequel, and had the best film noir collection of movies of anyone she knew. She crafted the best penises ever frosted, could do things with chocolate worthy of a centerfold and had once crafted a four-foot copy of Rodin's *The Kiss* out of Rice Krispies.

She rocked sex.

But the way she felt right this moment, she might as well have been a virgin schoolgirl.

Clumsy and clueless and totally out of her depth.

Before she could come up with something clever to say, he scraped his teeth over her throat. And sent huge, intense waves of pleasure crashing over her. Her knees shook. Her breath, too. She dug her fingers into his shoulders to keep herself steady. But the feel of those ripped muscles was too much.

She went crazy.

She drew her nails over his chest, wrapping one leg around his thigh. Vivian whimpered when the move pressed her damp core against his leg.

"Oh, God," she breathed, sliding up. Sliding down. Each slide made her tremble harder. "More. I have to have more."

She shoved at the fabric of his shirt to get to the skin beneath. A clever guy, he took the hint and tugged the shirt off over his head. The moment he tossed it aside, she clamped her teeth onto his shoulder while running her hands over all those amazing muscles.

"You have the most amazing body," she gasped.

"Preaching to the choir, sweetheart." He wrapped his hands around her waist, lifting her high enough for his mouth to latch on to her breast.

Heat exploded. His body wasn't the only thing that was amazing. His tongue. Oh, his tongue. He swirled, he laved, he licked. One nipple, then the other, then back again. Vivian's body was on fire. Her head dropped backward, hitting the door with a thud she barely heard over the sound of her own moans.

"The other room?" Zane ground the words between clenched teeth, his body so tense beneath her fingers that she was surprised he didn't explode.

She couldn't wait.

She wanted him to explode now.

"Here," Vivian insisted, staring into his eyes as she bit his lip. "Here and now."

"Oh, yeah," he breathed, his words somewhere between agreement and a reverent prayer of thanks before he took her mouth in a kiss hot enough to fry her brain cells.

Vivian was remotely aware of the rustling sound of foil ripping and gave a hum of approval she hoped he knew was gratitude since her mouth was too busy to voice the words.

With her body wedged between the door and Zane's powerful thighs, he gripped her butt in both hands and thrust.

Vivian exploded. The orgasm spiraled, spinning higher and higher and higher until she saw stars. Vivid, multicolored stars.

He pounded deep, each thrust sending her up again. She dug her heels into the rigid muscles of his butt, meeting each thrust with a whimper. Her head fell back against the door, her breath coming even faster than she was.

Oh. My. God.

Vivian's breath ripped from her lungs, leaving her throat burning and her heart on fire.

She'd thought she rocked sex.

She'd been so wrong.

As her heart slowly found its rhythm again, she tried

to gather a few of the scattered thoughts flying through her mind.

Awesome. Mind-blowing. Earth-shattering.

Vivian's eyes flew open, the breath she'd fought so hard to steady lodging in her chest like a boulder.

For her.

What about for him?

Zane was obviously a master. But now that she knew she was way out of her league, what'd that mean? Had he enjoyed it? Was he satisfied?

Slowly, hesitantly, she slid her hand over the rippling muscles of his back to rest just above his butt.

No sweat.

She frowned.

Why wasn't he sweaty?

Shouldn't door-banging sex make a guy sweat?

Sure, she wasn't sweaty. But it took a five-mile run on a hot day to even get a glow out of her, so that didn't count.

She'd wanted sex with Zane Bennett. Now she'd had it. What a lousy time to realize she wanted more.

More sex.

More orgasms.

More time.

More Zane.

She wanted to talk with him and hear about his adventures. She wanted to laugh at his jokes and learn his favorites.

She wanted everything.

But she wasn't supposed to want everything. She was supposed to be happy—thrilled, even—with hot sex.

Trying not to panic, Vivian let her legs slide down his until her feet found the floor. She felt Zane's groan rumble through her body before she heard it. Encouraged, she took a deep breath and put on her sexiest voice.

"How you doing, big boy?"

"Mmm." His hands still cupping her butt, he squeezed. "I'd say that was a pretty good start."

"Start?" Too surprised to be embarrassed anymore, she leaned back to stare into his face.

"Start," he confirmed, not even a little winded when he gave her a smile that melted her cacophony of fears and made her tingle all over again. "You said something about frosting?"

8

"He's amazing. Simply amazing."

"You said that. Like, twenty times already," Minna pointed out, most of her attention on the carrots she was peeling for her I'm-a-bride-and-have-to-fit-into-my-dress salad. "So why aren't you spending this evening with Mr. Amazing instead of me like you have the last four nights?"

"He's meeting up with his friends at the pub, then he said he probably had something to do. I'll see him tomorrow."

Tomorrow.

Adding a dash of Dijon to the balsamic and olive oil, she bit her lip to keep from giggling.

She would see Zane Bennett tomorrow. Just like she'd seen him every tomorrow since they'd damn near dented her front door. It was like a dream come true.

"It's not just sex, you know," she blurted out. Her hand froze on the jar of honey. "I mean, there is sex. Its amazing sex. But there's more. We talk. I told him all about my dreams for The Sweet Spot and he had a lot of great suggestions. He even knows someone in California who has an online bakery business. Apparently she started with cookies but does all sorts of stuff now. Not sexy stuff like I do, although he said she'd probably be totally awed by it. He offered to call her and see if she had any advice for me."

She went on to explain how Genna was the wife of one of his SEAL friends, and how she'd made a huge success of selling sweet treats online.

"Maybe you and this Genna can go into business together," Minna suggested. "Just think, you could get the internship, move to California and have a ready-made partner."

"I'd never move there. My home is here. My family is here. I have security here," she said, laughing as if the idea of leaving her hometown and family was totally ludicrous. "Besides, can you imagine me chasing after Zane all the way to California? He'd freak. I mean, I imagine he'd freak. But maybe he wouldn't. Maybe he'd want to keep seeing me. Not just because the sex is amazing—it is amazing. But we have something special between us."

She paused in the act of drizzling honey over the oil mixture to sigh.

"He's amazing. Not just because he's a SEAL, although, hellooo, sexy. But he's got this great attitude about everything. The way he talks about life, about his teammates, his challenges. It's so inspiring."

Last night, it'd inspired her to lick buttercream meringue icing off his pecs. Well, that and to update her website and Facebook page with photos of her latest cake creations.

"Viv. I was talking about the culinary internship. Not Zane."

"Oh. Right."

Whisking with all her might, Vivian stared at the bowl as if the answers to the universe were somewhere in the foam.

"Oh. My. God." Jabbing the carrot like a sword, Minna

shook her head. "You're getting gooey over the guy. What about your vow? The no-goo vow?"

"I'm not getting gooey." Vivian rolled her eyes as if the mere thought was ridiculous. But it wasn't. Because her emotions were heading fast and furious toward that sticky, icky, messy place that was goo.

"I think it's great," Minna declared, grabbing an apple from the bowl on Vivian's counter and dicing away, green peel and all. "Every woman needs to go to goo at least once in her life."

Since Zane got her going every time he smiled, Vivian figured she was covered for this and several more life-times.

"So other than the great sex, what's it like to date the great Zane Bennett?" Minna asked when they settled at the table, each with a huge salad and a glass of wine. "Does he take you to fancy restaurants or on long romantic drives? Or is he more a sporty date kind of guy?"

"Dates? Oh. Hmm." To give herself time, Vivian stabbed a big chunk of salad and chewed. "He took me for a ride on his Harley a couple of nights ago. We rode up to Lover's Peak."

"On a Harley?" Her fork halfway to her mouth, Minna froze in confusion. "How'd you do it on a Harley? Weren't you worried about the bike tipping over or something? Was the engine running?"

"Minna," she said, laughing. "We didn't do it on the motorcycle."

He'd had a blanket tucked in his saddlebag. "We sat on the ridge overlooking the lake and watched the stars. It was pure romance."

"Ohhh." Looking as if she was having fantasies no about-to-be-married woman should have, Minna sighed. "That sounds great. Where else have you gone?"

Where else?

Buying time, Vivian sipped her wine.

"I made him a candlelight dinner last night." And a chocolate-frosted dessert eaten off each other's naked bodies, topped with whipped cream. "The night before he stopped into the bakery to help me with another batch of chocolate candy."

It'd taken twenty minutes to clean all the chocolate off the stainless-steel table after he'd finger painted her naked body.

"Wow. Romantic and sweet," Minna said. Her gaze locked on her salad as if she were expecting a thousand extra calories to jump out of it, so she missed Vivian's frown.

Romantic and sweet. And private. Other than that first time for drinks, she realized they'd never gone anywhere public together.

"It's not just sex," Vivian said defensively. "I mean, yeah, we have a lot of sex. Great sex. Multiorgasmic sex. But that's not all we've got between us."

Was that all they had between them? That was all she'd intended to have between them. But now? Her stomach clenched against the sudden shaft of pain at the idea.

Vivian shook her head before Minna could voice the words to go along with her startled expression.

"It hasn't even been a week, so it's crazy to think it's, like, a relationship. But it is. We talk. We have tons in common. We like the same books, movies, music. He told me about a lot of the places he's seen. Oh, not the battles or secret stuff. Places like Japan and Bahrain and Cuba."

"I thought he lived in California."

"He's stationed there now, but he's had other assignments and sometimes just travels." Imagining how incredible it must be to see so much of the world, Vivian sighed. "Some of his teammates bring their wives, so they get to see the world, too."

"Viv—"

"I'm not crazy," Vivian interrupted before Minna could finish her squeaked protest. "Like I said, I know this is just sex. Still, he's great. Did I tell you that he helped me refine my business plan?"

They finished their salads and were well into dessert— baked apples with rum ice cream—by the time Vivian had finished outlining all of the great ideas they'd come up with.

"All I have to do is convince my parents to let me use the bakery kitchen when they're closed Sundays. Then I can put the evenings toward getting these ideas into play," she explained, swirling her spoonful of apple through the melting puddle of ice cream. "The Sweet Spot will be a success in no time. Talk about living the dream, right?"

"Uh-huh, right," Minna said, cutting off a fragment of cinnamon-spiced apple sans ice cream. "Not to crumble your cake or anything, but to use the professional tools, don't you currently have to sneak in kitchen time? Because, why?"

"Why?" Feeling a pout coming on, Vivian watched the ice cream dropping off her spoon. "Probably because I haven't pushed the issue. I mean, I've asked a lot. A few dozen times, maybe. But I haven't shown them my business plan."

Minna's stare lasted for a solid ten seconds before she shook her head and switched her healthy bowl of just apples for Vivian's ice cream and caramel-covered one.

"So, you and Zane," Minna said around a mouthful of sugary goodness. "There's a lot of romance?"

Nice subject change. Vivian frowned.

She debated either pushing the issue or, better, snagging her dessert back. But they both knew that even if she wrapped her business plan in a plain brown wrapper and had it presented by a nun, her parents were going to prude up. They would lecture, they would nag, they would heave great sighs of shame.

Was that why Zane didn't want to take her anywhere in public? Was he ashamed, too? Vivian chugged the last of her wine, scowling at the empty glass.

"How's Mike taking it?"

"Mike?" Mike could do no wrong in their parents' eyes. Of course, he'd inherited their prude gene, so he never tried.

"Yeah, Mike. I haven't heard about any recent hospitalization, but I've been pretty busy with my wedding prep, so I might have missed a thing or two." Minna rolled her eyes at Vivian's blank stare. "Do you really think your big brother would like the idea of his little sister with one of the Bad Boy Bennett brothers?"

"Ooooh, Mike."

Zane was hiding their relationship from Mike. Relief surged through Vivian so fast she felt dizzy. It wasn't shame that had Zane keeping things on the down low. He just didn't want to upset her brother.

That was so sweet. She'd never had a guy care like that. A guy who'd defy the bro code for her. Who'd worry about her family accepting him. For the first time, she realized that this thing between her and Zane wasn't a game. Wasn't just a way of making her favorite fantasy come true.

It was more than that, she admitted. She felt more. And— as terrifying as it was to even think—she wanted more.

Vivian took a deep breath and, freaking out a little because it was never easy to put her emotions out there, admitted, "I think you're right. I think I'm falling for Zane Bennett."

GUY'S GOTTA DO *what a guy's gotta do.*

And sometimes what a guy had to do simply sucked.

But Zane accepted this duty the same way he'd handled swabbing the head or KP when he was an ensign. By seeing it as a challenge. Something that, since he had to do it, he'd do damned well. Then, the minute it was over, he'd erase it from his memory.

Sitting next to a giant panther's paw, he rode down the street to the beat of "Party Like a Rock Star." His brother was on one side, Mike on the other, and their bros were lined up, shoulder to shoulder, under the panther's snarling head.

"This sucks," he said, not sure why he kept the comment under his breath when nobody could hear them over the music.

"Just kill me now," Xander said, his words pure disgust. "I knew we should have dismantled this thing. Or blown it up."

Mike elbowed him in the gut. "What'd he say?"

"Xander likes the panther," he lied diplomatically.

"You were supposed to be riding on that saddle up there," Mike pointed out. "We'd even lined up the local news to report on it and had a video crew doing a mini documentary."

Zane credited his navy training for keeping him from falling facedown off the float.

"I almost made it a challenge," Mike continued with a laugh. "But hey, you're already in the middle of trying to score with Quinn, right? Didn't seem right to double you up."

Thank God for Quinn.

Quinn.

Oh, shit. Zane scanned the crowd for the pretty brunette, tension still ripping through his shoulders even when he came up short of a sighting.

He hadn't seen her in a week. Not since they'd had coffee. And he'd been so off his game, he'd totally blown asking her out again. And he hadn't set foot in Myer's since that first night.

It wasn't that he'd forgotten about the challenge. Exactly. It was more that he'd been busy. Distracted. Focused. Yeah, focused. A guy had to have priorities, and the last few days with Vivian had required all of his attention.

Still, a challenge had been issued. And he owed it to himself—to his friends—to give it his all.

"Wasn't Quinn supposed to be part of the parade?" he asked Mike.

"Yeah, she was supposed to reprise her role as homecoming queen but she refused. Said she'd abdicated her crown years ago."

"Whoa, though," Mike said, leaning back and putting on his fake shocked face. "What's up with that? Shouldn't you have her schedule down solid by now? All her favorites memorized? A solid handle on the moves she likes, how to score and what it'll take to bring home the win?"

About to offer a snappy comment on how sad a guy would have to be to know all of that about a woman, let alone how tacky it was to play a woman like a ball game, Zane caught sight of Vivian through the crowd. Wearing a hot pink sundress with tiny straps and a tight waist, she leaned against the corner lamppost outside of the bakery, watching the parade go by.

She'd pulled her hair up into a ponytail with a fluffy bow that matched her dress, leaving her face unframed except for that sweep of bangs and the huge sunglasses she wore in defense of the bright morning light.

Pleasure surged as he relaxed into a smile, sending her

a special wink and a wave. Zane hadn't expected to see her. He hadn't even mentioned the parade. They didn't talk about the reunion events much. Partially because she wasn't really involved, although she'd mentioned a cake. But mostly because while he was grateful to the reunion for bringing him back into town, he was more interested in talking about Vivian.

Since he did know her schedule, he was surprised to see her out for the parade. She worked in the bakery kitchen from four in the morning until ten, then shifted to the front counter unless she had a heavy decorating schedule.

He knew her favorites, too. Red was her color, although turquoise was a close second. She loved chocolate, erotica and pushing the decorating envelope. Hated fake strawberry filling, pornography and something called basket weave, which he was pretty sure was some sort of frosting.

As for moves, she hadn't objected to a single one he'd made, he remembered with a grin. He'd scored enough to set new records—for both of them, thank you very much—and as for bringing home the win?

He smiled at Vivian again before she passed out of view and realized that she was it.

Vivian was his win.

Shit.

What was wrong with him?

Had the air gotten thinner all of a sudden? Zane tried to breathe, but couldn't quite find enough air to inflate his lungs.

He glanced at Xander. The guy was looking pretty damned satisfied but wasn't saying why. Zane had always been able to read his twin. But this time he couldn't tell was going on in Xander's head.

As if reading his thoughts, Xander glanced over. His ready smile faded at the look on Zane's face.

"You okay, man?" Xander frowned at him. "What's got you so stressed?"

"Challenges." Zane stared out at the crowd, forcing a smile as he waved to their sister and her two kids. "Dude, do you ever think we're too old for this crap?"

"The only ones who aren't too old for this crap are Joel and Teddy," he said, nodding at their nephews. Xander scowled at the panther as if he wanted to rip its head off with his bare hands and mount it on a wall. "And even that's a maybe."

Zane started to correct him, to explain that he meant the challenges, not the float. Dares were for kids. When did they cross the finish line to claim their adult status? he wondered as the float came to the end of the street and the parade wrapped up. They were navy SEALs. Wasn't it time to grow up?

"Dudes, bet you miss daily exercise, don't you?" Kyle greeted as they jumped off the float. "Wanna race to the auditorium? The senior center is serving up a pancake breakfast."

"I'm not running across the parking lot to get a stack of pancakes," Zane retorted.

"Bet I get there first," Lenny shouted, taking off at a run.

Zane and Xander exchanged eye rolls. Then they glanced down. Sneakers instead of dress shoes.

That meant, oh, yeah… It was on.

As one, they sprinted toward the pancakes.

9

TAKE A LITTLE candlelight, add some romantic music and a bottle of wine. What do you get?

The perfect evening.

Vivian danced across the room with a jiggly butt wiggle that she was pretty sure did amazing things for her skirt. Like make it cling to her hips in a very enticing way.

And enticing was job one on an anniversary. And twelve days counted as an anniversary when fourteen was the end.

She boogied her way into the kitchen to check the lasagna. Tangy sauce scenting the air? Check. Golden cheese bubbling? Check. Bread buttered and ready for broiling? Wine open and breathing? She glanced at the counter. Yep, ready.

She puffed out a deep breath, checked the straps of her halter dress and shook back her hair.

Ready.

She was so ready.

She heard the front door.

Woot. Talk about timing.

Almost skipping, she headed out of the kitchen, only to stop midhop in the doorway.

"Mike? What do you want?"

"Am I interrupting?" Brows raised, Mike made a show of eyeing the candlelit table. "Or am I *interrupting*? Got company, Viv?"

"No, but I will soon. So go away."

"Go away? Nah, I think I'll stick around." He dropped onto the couch, spreading his arms over the back cushions and propping his feet on the steamer trunk she used as a coffee table. "Smells like lasagna. You make a killer meal, Viv. Got extra?"

"Go away," Vivian said again, nudging his feet off the table. "Far, far away."

"But I'm so comfortable." He gave her a hopeful look.

"Why are you here?"

"You've got mail." He reached inside his jacket, then shook his head and pulled his empty hand free. "But what do I have? Bummer that it's not lasagna."

"You're going to have a thump on the head if you don't give me my mail, get off my couch and out of my living room." Vivian shifted from one foot to the other, then back again. She glanced at the door and nervously bit her lip. "Seriously. We're adults, Mike. Quit being an irritating big brother and go away."

"Fine, fine." Pushing to his feet, he held out a couple of envelopes, then lifted them high before Vivian could take them.

She ground her teeth to keep from screaming. What was the purpose of older brothers? The only thing keeping her from kneeing him in the groin and rolling his damaged body out the door was knowing that Zane would be here any second now.

"Michael," she said in her most threatening voice. "If you mess up my date, I'm going to hurt you."

"Who's the guy?" Her mail still in his hand, he wandered over to the table to scoop up a handful of sugared almonds, popping them one by one into his mouth. "Anyone I know?"

The knock on the door echoed through Vivian's head. *Uh-oh.*

Vivian used Mike's distraction to grab her mail just as the door opened. A quick flip showed a couple of bills, an equipment catalog, two lingerie magazines and an oversized manila envelope.

She wasn't sure if the sinking feeling in her stomach was from the look on her brother's face at the sight of Zane or from the Culinary Institute's return address on the large envelope.

"Yo, Bennett," Mike greeted Zane with a big grin and a slap on the back. "How'd you know where to find me?"

After a questioning look at Vivian, who only shrugged, Zane returned the greeting and sidestepped the question.

Content to be ignored for the moment, she stared at the envelope. Here it was. The answer to whether she was good enough, whether her designs were strong enough, whether her vision was focused enough to be worthy of pursuing.

Or, as her family always said, if she was just wasting her time. Catering to the crass, focusing on the tacky. Those and oh-so-many more phrases circled her brain as Vivian stared at the envelope.

Finally, she couldn't stand it any longer. A quick glance at the men assured her that they were deep in discussion about who might have decapitated the float head.

Heart trembling, she slowly, carefully slid her fingernail under the slit in the envelope, trying not to make a sound as she opened it.

She could have set it on fire for all the attention the men were paying to her, though. Realizing that, she pulled out the papers and read the cover letter.

Everything in her head went blurry.

"C'mon. Let's hit Myer's for a drink. We'll see you later, Viv."

Vivian blinked, bringing the pages back into focus when Mike's comment pulled her out of her shocked fog.

"What?" Sweeping her bangs aside to better frown at them. "You're leaving? Both of you?"

"Of course."

"Actually, I'm busy tonight," Zane said with a warm smile for Vivian.

Oh, yeah, he was. Vivian found her own smile as she imagined just how busy she planned for him to be. She had a gallon of fudge ripple and a bowl of homemade whipped caramel cream waiting.

"Too busy to hang out with the guys?" Mike demanded. "What could be more important than that? Besides, Vivian has a date."

He caught the look that passed between them.

"Whoa. Wait a second." Hand held high in denial, Mike glanced from Zane to Vivian and back again, then shook his head. "No way. You are not my sister's date."

It was rare to hear her brother in a temper, but that was definitely his pissed off voice.

Trying to think of a way to defuse the situation without ruining her evening, Vivian gulped back the knot of worry that was stuck in her throat.

Not for Zane. Not even with a crowbar could Mike put a dent in her SEAL.

Zane only shrugged and asked casually, "No?"

"That's my sister."

"Yeah. And you were the one who said that your sister can take care of herself."

Vivian blinked in surprise before pride trickled in, making her lift her chin and stiffen her spine. Yeah, she could.

"She can take care of herself with regular guys, sure. Most of them are scared of her."

What? Her chin dropped again, this time in shock. Who was afraid of her? Well, Lenny was, but he didn't count. He was afraid of anything with breasts. Kyle could never look her in the eye, but that was because his were always *on* her breasts.

Of course, they were good breasts, she admitted to herself when she saw Zane checking them out. Especially when showcased by the square neckline of her favorite floral dress.

"What the hell, dude? I thought you were romancing Quinn Oswald. Why are you here with my sister?"

What? Vivian stopped running her fingers along the edge of her bodice.

"I never said I was romancing Quinn," Zane denied with a shake of his head.

"The hell you didn't."

"Let's review, shall we? If you recall, my exact words were that I was romancing someone very special. You assumed that meant Quinn."

Awww. Vivian actually felt her heart melt into a big puddle of goo at his words. It took a little effort, but she managed to ignore it. Because she wanted to know what the hell Quinn had to do with anything.

Apparently her brother knew. The vein in Mike's forehead was pulsing and he looked ready to punch the hell out of Zane.

"I assumed that because of the challenge."

"What challenge?"

Squaring off like a pair of dogs over a bone, the men both ignored Vivian's question.

"And what about the bro code?" Mike yelled, waving

his arms in the air like a duck losing altitude. "Did you ask my permission before dating my sister?"

"Who are you to give me permission to date?"

They ignored that, too, as Zane laughed off Mike's argument like it was as lame as the duck flapping.

"You waived the bro code. You even said your sister could take care of herself."

Oh. Vivian stood a little straighter, her smile filled with pride. She'd never realized her brother had so much faith in her.

"She's my sister," Mike shouted, as if that was enough of a reason. "And you're dating Quinn."

Her smile disappeared, stunned pain replacing pride.

"Dating—" She couldn't get the words past the roaring in her head. Zane was dating? Dating another woman? Quinn Oswald? He was dating the perfect woman? Vivian's breath hitched.

"You've been romancing Quinn Oswald?" She hugged her arms tight. "Pikes Peak's Princess?"

Not only pretty, but sweet and friendly and, according to all of the rumors, the goal of every single man in town.

And Zane was chasing after her? Vivian's vision blurred into a haze of fury.

"Out," she snapped, pointing at the door.

"Vivian, let me explain."

"Not you," she told Zane, slapping her hand on his chest. "Mike. Out. Now."

"Viv—"

"Go." Since words weren't doing the job, she added a nice shove to get her brother moving. Then, his protests still echoing, she slammed and locked the door.

The same door Zane had first taken her against, she remembered, drawing in a shaky breath.

"I'm sorry about that. It's no big deal," he said, grabbing the bottle of wine and pouring a hefty portion. "You know Mike, the guys, they're always issuing these challenges. Like drag racing down Main, jumping off the gym roof, dancing on the cafeteria table."

He offered her the glass and what she assumed was an attempt at a charming smile.

Vivian didn't accept either.

"Those were in high school, Zane. High school was ten years ago for you."

"A challenge is a challenge," he defended, looking fierce. "A man can't walk away from a challenge. C'mon, Vivian, it's no big deal. You know Mike, Lenny, Kyle and the gang. They're idiots about this kind of thing. You can't really be upset about it, can you?"

He held out the glass again. This time, Vivian took it, carried it to the sink and, her eyes locked on his, poured it straight down. Something flashed in Zane's eyes, but she was too angry to try to decipher it.

"I take that as a yes."

"Yes, Zane. You should definitely take it as a yes, I'm upset."

"You shouldn't be. It's not like I'm interested in Quinn."

Vivian drew in a long, slow breath between clenched teeth, then asked, "Did you take her out? Did you actually date her?"

Zane's hesitation was infinitesimal, but she caught it.

So she shouldn't have been surprised when he admitted, "It was just coffee."

"Just coffee. But you're not interested. Yet you're dating her anyway." Vivian's lower lip trembled, her heart—the one she'd been so sure wasn't at risk—feeling like he'd just drop kicked it out the window. "So that makes me, what? The consolation prize?"

"No, c'mon, Vivian. Don't make this into something it

isn't. I'm not sleeping with Quinn. I'm not even interested in her like that."

But Vivian caught it. The unspoken something at the end of that sentence.

"You're going to keep going with this stupid challenge, aren't you?"

Zane looked baffled, as if she'd asked him if he was actually going to save the drowning puppy.

"Of course. A challenge was extended, I accepted. I can't back down. I never back down."

"You're not backing out of this challenge," she realized, sinking onto the couch. She rubbed her hand over her forehead before meeting his eyes again.

"You don't get it," he said with a smile, sitting opposite her. "This is who I am. Meeting challenges, facing the difficult, it's what I do."

"What you choose to do."

"Yes. Because that's how I achieve things. That's how I make them happen. You keep talking about what you want to do, about your dream of building your business, right? How is that not a challenge?"

"That's different."

Zane reached across the table to take her hand in his.

"How?" he asked, nibbling on one finger, then the next. "What's the difference? You want something, right? In this case, your career. In my case, to uphold my rep."

He scraped his teeth over her finger, sparking a flash of desire deep in her belly, before he swirled his tongue along the side. Vivian bit her lip to keep from moaning.

"You want to make your career rock, Vivian. Then step up and do it. Reach out and take it."

He gave her finger one last nip, nibbled his way up her wrist. Vivian's breath came a little faster as he slid his lips over her shoulder, then whooshed out when he buried his mouth in the crook of her neck.

"I want it," she admitted with a low moan. "I really do."

His fingers skimmed her breasts, dipping and teasing their way over the edge of her bodice.

"Are you willing to work for it?" he asked, his words low and husky in her ear. "To take risks for it? To put it all on the line to have it?"

God, yes.

She'd give anything to have it right now. To strip it bare, to climb on and ride it for all it was worth. She'd milk every drop of satisfaction from it.

Her breath shook with the tiny orgasm rippling through her body.

"It feels good, doesn't it?"

Vivian's eyes fluttered open to focus on Zane's face. Those sexy eyes and that wicked smile. God, he was gorgeous. She couldn't remember ever feeling so good, so amazing. Staring at Zane, she realized it wasn't just the orgasm. It was the feeling she got being around him.

"It feels amazing," she admitted, wishing they were talking about the same thing.

"You want to make your dream come true, move to Southern California," he suggested, nibbling on her knuckles now. "There are hundreds of specialty bakeries in the area. SoCal is the entertainment capital of the world. There's no place that'd appreciate erotic desserts more, except maybe Las Vegas."

Vivian opened her mouth but nothing came out. Probably because all the air had been sucked away, leaving her gasping.

"Say I move to California," she managed. "Would I see you again?"

"See me?" He laughed. "Babe, you make the best cupcakes I've ever tasted. You'd see me all the time."

Oh, boy, there it was.

All her dreams, right there on a gorgeous platter.

Vivian's lips trembled into a hesitant smile, her heart
racing with excitement.

He loved her cupcakes.

Wait.

Cupcakes.

She wet her lips.

"Did you take her one of my cupcakes?"

10

"In order to romance Quinn Oswald into a date, did you take her one of my cupcakes?"

"What?"

Vivian tried to ignore the kick-in-the-gut pain, but it was stealing her breath.

"You did, didn't you?"

For the first time since he'd walked in the door, Zane looked uncomfortable.

"Look, we're not talking about cupcakes."

"No." Vivian pulled her hand away and pushed off the couch. "We're talking about challenges. Something you'll apparently take at any cost."

"You're holding out for guarantees, clinging to your safety net. And you accuse me of having a problem?" Zane shook his head. "The only way to grow is to take risks, Vivian. If you want something, you have to be willing to pay the price to get it."

"And in this case, the price you're willing to pay is us," Vivian shot back, refusing to hear what she knew he was saying.

"C'mon, Vivian. You don't actually expect me to walk away from a challenge, do you?"

She wanted to ask him to do it for her. She wanted to tell him that while it didn't mean anything to him, and it might not even mean anything to Quinn, it meant something to her. It would mean that she was important to him. That she mattered.

Dammit, it'd mean he cared. He wanted her to walk away from her safety net. All she had to do was risk everything, put it all on the line. All of her dreams. The career dreams, the relationship dreams. Everything.

What if she failed?

Her stomach wrapped itself into knots so tight she could barely breathe.

"Look, Vivian—"

No. She didn't want to hear it. She didn't want to know she was great, but not quite great enough. She didn't want to hear that she was special, if only she'd change one little thing or the other.

"You should go."

"Look, let's eat that delicious lasagna and talk this through."

Vivian stalked into the kitchen, grabbed the lasagna off the counter, shoved it into his hands, then waved her arm.

"Please go." She jabbed her finger toward the door. "I'm sure you have a date, or whatever."

"Viv."

"Look, I'm starting to fall for you. So go, please, before I actually finish the fall."

Zane's mouth dropped open. He closed it. Before he could voice the shock—or panic, or both—that was clear on his face, she did the unthinkable.

She cried.

She managed to keep it to a single tear, but it was enough to get him out the door.

And all she could think was *Oh, God*. Had she actually said that?

Vivian stared at the closed door for so long that her eyes burned. But no amount of denial could change the facts.

She'd just told Zane Bennett, the hottest guy she'd ever known, that she was falling in love with him.

Vivian groaned.

First that letter. Now this?

Could this night get any worse?

PANIC SLAMMED THROUGH Zane's system. Lasagna in hand, he stared at the closed door. At least he thought it was panic. He'd never panicked before in his life, so he might be wrong. But remembering the single tear glisten a silvery track down Vivian's cheek, he didn't think so.

An hour later, Zane still felt like shit.

He'd finished off the entire lasagna, which had been unquestionably delicious, but could have used a little garlic bread to sop up the sauce.

Now he sat at the small jut of Formica Lenny called a kitchen table with a full stomach, wondering what the hell had happened. He debated finding his cell phone, calling Xander. Or Lansky. Or maybe he could try Vivian again.

But three calls after she'd told him to get out of her apartment was probably too much.

"Zane, what are you doing here?"

"I was craving bad coffee." He lifted the mug that claimed that This Is What a War Machine Looks Like. "What are you doing here? I thought you had a hot date."

"I did, we did, now it's done." Grabbing a beer, Lenny dropped into the torn chair opposite him and took a mouthful. "Hottest fifteen minutes of her night, let me tell you."

"My man." Zane toasted him with his mug. "You sure know how to rock the ladies of Little Creek."

"How about you? I thought you had plans tonight."

"They changed." Changed, were changed. Whatever.

"Not hanging with Xander?"

"Nah." Not for lack of trying, but his brother wasn't answering his phone. Odd.

Xander would be the perfect person to hang with right now. The man had insights. He had the skills to dig beyond the surface of an issue and find the core problem. Not that Zane needed anyone to point out where he'd screwed up. He was pretty clear on that. But how to fix it? That part was a little murky.

Zane pulled out his phone to scowl at the blank display. Where the hell was Xander when he needed him?

Zane looked across the table at his brother's stand-in. The lanky, freckled boy next door whose greatest ambition was to own the gas station where he worked. As far as Zane could remember, the guy had dated two women, so his expertise was nothing to brag about. And the one he'd married had kicked his butt to the curb months ago.

That didn't mean he didn't have anything to offer.

"Do you think I'm incapable of refusing a challenge?"

"Why would you bother? That's how you prove you've still got it, my friend."

Zane blinked. What the hell? He was a SEAL. He disposed of live bombs for a living. He jumped out of planes, dived into oceans and, dammit, pounded sixty-four-ounce slushies in a single gulp.

Why did he have to prove anything?

"Dude, you and Xander, you're like our heroes. You guys live the dream. Kicking ass, saving the world."

"If you think that ass-kicking and world-saving are so great, why the idiotic dares when we come home?"

"How else would we get you back here?" Twisting off

the cap of another beer, Lenny laughed. "Like you're gonna come back to hang out with your boring old buddies?"

"We come back all the time," Zane said, dismissively. "Our family lives here. We're not going to stop visiting."

"Visiting Little Creek, sure. But us? Most of the guys are married. Joe has a kid on the way. Sure, I'm holding down the fort as the hottest bachelor in town, but let's get real, you're not coming back to play my wingman." Lenny laughed so hard he snorted beer. "As if."

Huh.

Good point.

Ten minutes later, Lenny had gone to his room to pass out, leaving Zane to contemplate his friend's buck-toothed brilliance. Well, that and leave another message for Xander.

Where the hell was his brother?

Zane stepped out to sit on the narrow excuse for a patio that ran between Lenny's apartment and Vivian's and contemplated one of the biggest challenges he'd ever faced.

Figuring out what to do about this situation with Vivian.

On one hand, his career as a SEAL was based on challenges. Every training session, every op, every mission was a new challenge to be faced. And damned if he didn't rock them, every one. Because that was what he did.

Which brought him to his other hand.

Was he so incapable of refusing a challenge that he'd let that blow his shot with a woman as great as Vivian? Was his ego more important than her feelings?

Which brought him to her feelings.

She'd said she might be falling.

Zane's spine twitched as something that resembled panic started climbing up his back again.

Falling?

Wasn't that his signal to start running?

Sure, he'd wanted her to move to San Diego, to live near him. He'd pictured them continuing the fun and games. Great sex, lots of laughs, more sex, good times and, yeah, more sex. And sure, they had a lot more going on than that. Other than the challenge thing, which she clearly didn't understand the importance of, she totally got him. She made him feel great. And he'd thought he did the same for her.

But falling?

That was serious.

What if it didn't work? What is she moved there and wasn't happy? What if they failed as a couple?

Talk about challenges.

It was better this way, he decided. Her brother had said to get out. She'd said to get out. He'd gotten out.

Mike would see that as honoring the bro code.

Vivian would see it as doing exactly as she'd asked.

And he could finish out the challenge and, yeah, even though he'd pretty much ignored it until now, he could pull off a win.

All he had to do was accept that it was over with Vivian.

"Yo, VIV?"

Vivian bit her lip against the urge to scream, but didn't bother looking up from the cake she was decorating. She'd come in early to finish this cake hoping she wouldn't have to talk to anyone. Was this Mike's challenge? To ruin every one of her plans?

"This is a bad time," she said quietly. "I'm working."

"So? You can work and talk at the same time."

Because it took no focus or talent to slap frosting on a cake? Vivian whipped her whisk through melted sugar then flicked it over the rack, where it hardened instantly in slender, misty strands of gold.

"About this deal with Zane."

"I don't want to talk about it." Moving around the table, she spun sugar over two more racks. "Was there anything else? Because I have to finish this cake."

"I didn't realize you and Zane were a thing."

"Is that the new term for *consolation prize*?"

"C'mon, Viv. You should give Zane a chance. He's really upset about what happened."

He was? Vivian's hand froze midflick. Maybe she should talk to him. Apologize and explain why she'd been so over-the-top the night before.

She set the bowl aside and turned to stare at her brother.

"Just, you know, let him finish the challenge first."

"Finish the challenge?" Vivian bit back a scream. "You are saying you want me to get together with your friend, but he has to win this little bet first? The bet that involves him dating another woman?"

And this from a man who thought she was too risqué because she decorated penis cakes?

"No, of course not. He doesn't have to win a bet. It's not like there's money riding on it. And Xander has just as good a shot. But they have to finish it. It's a tradition."

A tradition.

Vivian drew in a deep breath through her nose, hoping the air would cool the fire in her gut. When it didn't, she grabbed her bottle of water and guzzled. That, and another breath were enough for her to be able to look her brother in the face and say, calmly, "Some traditions are stupid."

Needing to finish the cake, so ready to be done with everything—especially the confusion—she grabbed a sugar burst.

"Sometimes *tradition* is just another word for *limiting*. For staying in a rut. Some traditions are excuses to never take risks, never change, never try." Vivian bit her lip, all of her attention on placing the final explosion of sugar on the top of the cake so it poured like fireworks out of the panther's paws. "This bakery is all about traditions, isn't it?"

"Of course. Three generations of bakers. That's something to be proud of. Something to be respected, even."

"It is." And it was something she'd forgotten in her determination to pursue her own dreams. "You're right. Sometimes traditions matter."

Clearly traditions mattered to Zane.

And obviously traditions mattered to her family. And, she could now see, they mattered to her. So much so that she'd never follow her dreams if she stayed here in Little Creek. She'd keep glomming on to excuses. She'd keep sabotaging herself.

This thing with Zane had made her realize one thing. She couldn't face her own challenge if she kept hiding behind traditions.

"You're right," she said again. "And my designs go against that tradition, don't they? I'll talk to Mom and Dad when they get home tomorrow."

"Excellent. You're going to tell them you're done with that crazy baking stuff?"

She thought of the acceptance letter from the culinary institute.

"No. I'm going to tell them that they need to find a baker to replace me. I'm moving to California to intern with one of the great dessert chefs in the culinary field."

"What? No," Mike protested. "You can't do that."

"Sure I can." Vivian toured the cake, walking around to check it from all sides before deeming it finished. That gave her enough time to gauge the nerves dancing in her belly and decide if they were good and happy or bad and freaked out.

A little bit of each, she decided, whipping off her apron and exchanging it for her purse.

"Where do you think you're going?"

"I don't think, I know." She picked up a pink cardboard box sporting The Sweet Spot's sticker. "I'm going to talk with Zane."

"No." Mike shoved to his feet, scurried across the room and stood in front of the door, arms crossed over his chest. "You're not interfering."

"Yes. I am." Vivian angled sideways, heading for the back door instead. She had it open before he managed to uncross his arms. "Oh, and before I talk with Zane? I'm going to fill Quinn in on your little challenge. Just so it's fair."

She left to the sound of her brother's scream of protest.

Ten minutes later, she'd tracked down Quinn's place and knocked on the door. When the brunette answered, Vivian choked back the automatic surge of envy at how gorgeous the woman was.

"Hi, I'm Vivian. I was hoping we could chat." She lifted the box and smiled. "I brought cupcakes."

"Hi, Vivian," Quinn greeted with a hesitant smile. "Why?"

"First, because I love your boots and figure any woman who has such great taste in footwear is one I'd like to know. Second, I know you grew up here, but you haven't been back long so I thought maybe you could use a friend. And third—" she lifted the lid to show off the variety pack of cupcakes "—some things are better discussed with sugar."

11

ZANE HAD NEVER felt less like partying than he did right at that moment. But obligations were like duty. You reported whether you wanted to or not.

So, wearing slacks and a black shirt, no tie—because, dammit, he refused to wear his uniform—Zane strode into the country club to the blast of "Fergalicious." It was like stepping back in time to the prom. The gilt and marble ballroom was filled with balloons, streamers, paper panthers and overdressed people fighting to impress each other.

Thankfully, this was the final reunion event. The luncheons and ceremonies and parades were over. After tonight's reunion dance, it was all finished.

Once, he'd have seen this as his duty to liven the party up, to make an impression. Now? He glanced at his watch, gauging how much time he had to put in before he could try to reach Vivian again.

He'd gone by her apartment, he'd stopped in at the bakery, he'd even checked with Mike. Unless a bizarre lecture on the importance of traditions counted for anything, it'd been a total bust.

Zane made his way through the dancing crowd, a handful of chatting groups, a few people passing a flask and the half-dozen couples making out in the corners.

It really was like prom.

Which, if he remembered correctly, had included a group skinny-dipping dare that had gotten half the graduating class put into detention.

Who'd have thought that he'd be here, ten years older and a decorated Navy SEAL, and just as stupid. More than ready to have this evening and the reminder of his mistakes finished, Zane looked around for his buddies.

He spotted his brother first, standing by the piano watching the entrance.

"Yo," he greeted when he reached Xander. "Great party, right?"

Xander nodded in greeting, a troubled expression in his eyes. "You look like hell."

"Thanks, man. Glad to know you've always got my back."

"Always."

They stood there in silence for a few minutes, watching their past dancing around to Beyoncé's "Irreplaceable." Which was fine until Mrs. Marshall, their old algebra teacher, started gyrating against the gym teacher, Mr. Bridges.

"Oh, man," Zane breathed in horror.

"So wrong," Xander agreed.

"We're supposed to find Kyle," Zane said when they tore their eyes away.

"Right." Xander sighed. "Challenge time, and all that."

"Yeah. All that." Zane frowned as he studied his brother. He hadn't seen much of him the last few days, but it didn't take that mythical twin thing to know there was something wrong. "You okay?"

"Why wouldn't I be?"

Zane could think of dozens of reasons, none of which

Xander seemed open to hearing. Since he recognized that closed look on his brother's face, he went the opposite direction.

"Can I ask you something?"

"You want advice? Did you bump your head?"

Before Zane could respond, they were descended upon by a loud, rowdy group of locusts better known as their buddies. Only Mike appeared less than jubilant. Instead, he stood off to the side with a closed expression on his face.

"Challenge time," Kyle called out again, raising his hand in the air for a high five. Zane exchanged looks with Xander, and taking comfort from knowing someone else was hating this as much as he was, let someone else step up to return the hand slap.

"So which one of you are here with Quinn?" Lenny asked. "I've got twenty riding on this. If I can collect before the next song, I can snag a date for the rest of the party."

"Who scored?" Kyle demanded.

"Not me." Zane lifted one hand, fingers curved to reflect that zero.

"I'm here alone," Xander said with a shrug.

You'd think they'd told the gang they'd decided to leave the Navy to join an all-male pink-tutu-wearing burlesque troupe. All of their faces drooped, their jaws dropped, their collective gasp blew through the room like a hurricane.

Kyle grabbed a chair.

Lenny grabbed a beer.

Mike glared while Joe started babbling about failure, bubbles bursting and panther pride.

"Okay, so neither of you could bring in the win," Kyle finally managed. "But we have to declare a winner. So who was closest to a date tonight?"

"Cupcake," Lenny burst out. "Zane scored a cupcake."

Cupcake and coffee, actually.

A challenge was on the line. His honor. His rep.

A movement across the room caught his eye. A flash of red satin, black leather and a very tall cake shaped like a panther. *Vivian.*

"Gotta go," he said, clapping his brother on the shoulder. "I've got a lady to see about a cake."

VIVIAN SKIMMED ONE hand down her hip, smoothing the satin. She was slightly overdressed for a class reunion, but she was okay with that.

Because she was a woman on a mission.

And her mission was standing over there with his crew, looking about as hot as hot could get.

Vivian took one second to revel in the awe and admiration of the crowd as they gathered around the cake, everyone blown away by the awesomeness that was a four-foot-tall glittering black panther wearing a Pikes Peak High letterman's jacket.

"It's perfect."

"It's too perfect."

Zane caught her eye, his expression intense enough to give her shivers all the way across the room. But when he started walking her way, a part of her wanted to run in the other direction. Maybe she shouldn't be here.

"We can't cut unto that."

"Of course you can cut into it." Vivian grabbed the cake knife, whapping off the foot. "There, see."

Ignoring the shocked faces, she scooted out from behind the dessert table. She was tempted to wipe her damp palms on her dress, but it was satin. Which, she reminded herself, was why she'd worn it. Well, that and because it did a great job of highlighting her figure.

Something she was pleased to see Zane was taking note of.

Still, not even the heated appreciation in his eyes was enough to assuage her nerves.

"Hi."

"Hi," Vivian said, just a little breathless. Not out of desire this time, although she was trembling a little being this close to him.

Or was it her dream, standing right there in front of her looking so damned fine?

"Do you mind?" Zane asked, one second before he slid his arms around her waist. Before Vivian could ask, "Mind what," he leaned down to take her mouth in a kiss that made her toes curl. Her fingers dug into his shoulders for balance, but just as she was sinking into the kiss, he pulled away.

"Hi," she murmured again, making him smile.

"Yo, everyone," Zane called out to the room in general. He gave it long enough for a handful of people to look over. "Have you met Vivian? My date for the evening?"

"What?"

"Dammit."

"But, dude, the challenge?"

Ignoring the complaints and comments of his friends, Zane led Vivian out to the relative privacy of outdoors. Hands entwined, they walked along a rose-scented balcony gleaming with fairy lights.

Now that she had him alone, though, Vivian wasn't sure what to say. She'd planned the evening so carefully. The dress, the shoes, her hair and makeup. She'd rehearsed her hello, she'd practiced the walk across the room a half-dozen times.

But now? Standing there staring at the man of her dreams? She realized that she had no clue what to do next.

Should she say she'd overreacted to a simple cupcake situation, blowing it all out of proportion because she was scared of her own feelings?

Did she tell him she'd quit her job at the bakery and accepted the internship in San Diego at the Culinary Institute?

Did she vow undying love?

"I walked away from the challenge," Zane said.

"Oh." Vivian bit her lip. "Is it crazy to say that's one of the most romantic things I've ever heard?"

Zane laughed.

"No crazier than it was for me to keep trying to prove a pointless point." He gave a head shake and a self-derisive grimace. "It was ridiculous of me to put something that didn't matter to me over *someone* who does."

Oh. Vivian's heart finished the fall, tumbling right there at his feet. She wanted to grab on to now and run with it, but she had to put the truth out there.

"I don't want you to think I'm chasing after you or anything. But I am moving to California. I was offered the internship—"

Before she could finish what was feeling like a confession, Zane had let out a loud whoop. He grabbed her waist and swung her around in a circle.

"I knew you could do it. I told you could kick sexy cake butt."

"You did say that. And you were right. I was afraid to take that final step," she admitted. "As much as I talk a good game, a part of me is still the shy little girl who wants to hide in the corner because she's afraid someone is going to point out that she doesn't belong at the party with the cool kids."

"I guess that means I'm one of the cool kids?"

"As one of the Bad Boy Bennett brothers, you are the king of the cool kids." To back up her point, she gestured to one of the poster-sized framed portraits propped on a tripod just inside the glass doors. "Look at you. All sexy and heroic in your uniform."

Zane glanced over, grimaced and shook his head.

"That's Xander."

"What?" Horrified, Vivian started over to take a closer look. She only needed one step and a glance at the grin on Zane's face to know he was teasing.

"Kidding. That's me," he said, laughing. "You know, it's crazy. Xander and I aren't identical, but half the people out there can't tell us apart."

"Is Xander as addicted to challenges as you are?" she wondered as she saw Quinn step into the ballroom looking like a prom queen.

"I wouldn't say addicted."

Uh-huh. Vivian's mouth pursed in a surprised *O* before she pressed her lips together to hide her smile.

"What would you say if he won the latest one?"

After giving her one long, narrow look, Zane glanced over his shoulder just in time to see his brother kissing Quinn. His grin was all the answer Vivian needed.

"I'd say go, Xander," he said, turning back to give Vivian an intense look. "But I'm not a sore loser. It's not the winning that really matters. It's just that I thrive on challenges. On pushing myself and striving to be stronger. That's part of what's made me a SEAL."

"No." Vivian shook her head. "What makes you a SEAL is your dedication. Your talent. Your determination and your skill. That's who you are, Zane. It's who you've always been."

"So no more challenges?"

"Well, no more that involve other women," she said with a look that said that should be obvious. "But if the intense demands of being a SEAL aren't enough for you, I wrote down a few dozen ideas to challenge you with. Some involve frosting, two involve ice and there might be a few that require special toys."

Vivian felt all her nerves disappear as Zane's laughter washed over her.

"So about that fall you mentioned the other night," he murmured.

Uh-oh, here comes the nerves again. Vivian tried to swallow but her mouth was too dry.

"About that. I know it's too soon. I know it's crazy."

"I love you, Vivian."

"Oh." She blinked. "Oh, man. I so love you, too."

Sliding his hands into her hair, he took her mouth in a kiss hot enough to turn her knees into mush. Vivian had to grab on to his shoulders to keep from sinking to the ground. And, better yet, to keep from pulling him down on top of her.

"You're sure about moving to California?" he asked quietly, his fingers sliding through her hair, soothing her with each caress. "It's going to be a big change."

"It'll be a big change and there will be big risks," Vivian acknowledged, laying her head on his shoulder as she glanced back into the ballroom. "There's so much that I'll miss. The people. The comfort of working in a place I really like and know I'm good at. And, I suppose, the safety of it all."

Nerves danced in her belly, gyrating back and forth between excitement and terror. She gave it a second to decide which was stronger, then lifted her head to meet Zane's eyes.

"But you know what? Whatever happens, I'm ready for it. I'm excited to dive in and do the work to make my dreams come true."

"And me?"

"I'm even more excited to dive in and do you," she teased, her fingers twining together behind his neck as Zane took her mouth in a kiss made for a romance novel.

* * * * *

Dear Reader,

I first met *New York Times* bestselling author Tawny Weber online fifteen years ago when we were both unpublished writers seeking our first sales. Deciding to become critique partners, we emailed each other often, but it wasn't until we met face-to-face at RWA's national conference in Dallas over two years later that we really clicked. Right then and there, a friendship was born!

Despite the many, many miles between us (2,639 miles to be exact, but who's counting?) we became the best of friends, and I honestly couldn't imagine my life without her. Throughout the years we've read and critiqued each other's work, brainstormed ideas for stories and helped each other with career planning. So when the opportunity to actually write a book together arrived, I jumped at the chance.

I'm so glad I did. I had such fun writing *All In* and I know *One Night with a SEAL* will always hold a special place in my heart because Tawny and I created it together.

I hope you enjoy Xander and Quinn's stories. And if you can't get enough of those sexy SEALs (and let's be honest, who can?) don't forget to check out Team Poseidon in Tawny's new SEAL Brotherhood series, published by HQN Books.

Please visit my website, bethandrews.net, to check out all my titles, or drop me a line at beth@bethandrews.net. I'd love to hear from you.

Happy reading!
Beth Andrews

FREE Merchandise is 'in the Cards' for you!

Dear Reader,

We're giving away FREE MERCHANDISE!

Seriously, we'd like to reward you for reading this novel by giving you **FREE MERCHANDISE** worth over $20 retail. And no purchase is necessary!

You see the Jack of Hearts sticker above? Paste that sticker in the box on the Free Merchandise Voucher inside. Return the Voucher today... and we'll send you Free Merchandise!

Thanks again for reading one of our novels—and enjoy your Free Merchandise with our compliments!

Pam Powers

Pam Powers

P.S. Look inside to see what Free Merchandise is **"in the cards"** for you!

W

e'd like to send you two free books like the one you are enjoying now. Your two books have a combined cover price of over $10 retail, but they are yours to keep absolutely FREE! We'll even send you 2 wonderful surprise gifts. You can't lose!

REMEMBER: Your Free Merchandise, consisting of **2 Free Books** and **2 Free Gifts**, is worth over $20 retail! No purchase is necessary, so please send for your Free Merchandise today.

Get TWO FREE GIFTS!

We'll also send you 2 wonderful FREE GIFTS (worth about $10 retail), in addition to your 2 Free books!

Visit us at:

www.ReaderService.com

YOUR FREE MERCHANDISE INCLUDES...
2 FREE Books **AND** 2 FREE Mystery Gifts

FREE MERCHANDISE VOUCHER

2 FREE BOOKS and **2 FREE GIFTS**

Please send my Free Merchandise, consisting of **2 Free Books** and **2 Free Mystery Gifts**. I understand that I am under no obligation to buy anything, as explained on the back of this card.

225/326 HDL GLTD

Please Print

FIRST NAME

LAST NAME

ADDRESS

APT.#

CITY

STATE/PROV.

ZIP/POSTAL CODE

Offer limited to one per household and not applicable to series that subscriber is currently receiving.
Your Privacy—The Reader Service is committed to protecting your privacy. Our Privacy Policy is available online at www.ReaderService.com or upon request from the Reader Service. We make a portion of our mailing list available to reputable third parties that offer products we believe may interest you. If you prefer that we not exchange your name with third parties, or if you wish to clarify or modify your communication preferences, please visit us at www.ReaderService.com/consumerschoice or write to us at Reader Service Preference Service, P.O. Box 9062, Buffalo, NY 14240-9062. Include your complete name and address.

NO PURCHASE NECESSARY!

HD-517-FM17

ALL IN

Beth Andrews

Tawny—this one's for you!

1

"LOOKING FOR TROUBLE, SAILOR?"

The husky female voice somehow floated above the din of Myer's Pub, rising above the conversations and laughter, the sharp crack of pool balls and even the thumping bass of the rock song blaring from the corner jukebox.

Then again, Xander Bennett was a SEAL, one of the military's elite. He'd been trained to notice what others missed. To be alert, always, and so in tune with his surroundings, he could predict what was going to happen before it occurred.

Or maybe it was because when it came to Quinn Oswald, he'd always been like a goddamn lapdog, hyperaware of where she was, what she was doing, and pathetically eager to be noticed, to be given any scrap of attention.

He turned, kept the move slow and easy, his expression clear. He'd known she was here. His sister, Kerri, had told him Quinn was back in their hometown and working at Myer's. Plus, it'd been years—ten to be exact—since high school and his deeply hidden, long-seated infatuation with her. Seeing her now in this dim, cramped bar, being close enough to touch her, to breathe in her scent, shouldn't affect him.

And it sure as hell shouldn't feel like he'd taken the butt end of an AK-47 to the chest.

Then again, she'd always had the ability to steal his breath.

He dropped his gaze, took his time working his way from her high-heeled, short boots, up long, shapely legs encased in tight denim, over rounded hips and a narrow waist. Her black tank top ended at her belly button, baring two inches of flat stomach, before clinging to her ample breasts, the wide straps showing off her tanned shoulders and long neck.

And then he reached her face. Quinn Oswald had only improved with age.

Damn her.

She'd cut her hair. No longer did it fall to the middle of her back, but swung above her shoulders, the dark tresses a sharp contrast to the blue of her eyes. Her face had narrowed somewhat, making her high cheekbones more prominent, her mouth fuller.

Christ, but he used to fantasize about that mouth. About those lips wrapped around him.

His body stirred and as he watched, Quinn smiled, slow and confident. A woman certain in her ability to bring a man to his knees. A woman who knew what a man thought about when he looked at her. What he wanted.

Shit.

He held her gaze. "Actually, it's Lieutenant. And I don't look for trouble."

"No," she said, thoughtfully, that knowing smile still playing on her lips. "You wouldn't. *Lieutenant*."

Xander narrowed his eyes. What the hell did that mean?

"But your brother," she continued, lifting her chin toward the far corner of the bar. "Now, he's a different story, isn't he?"

He turned. Zane, his fraternal twin, sat with his back against the wall—all the better to protect himself and keep an eye on everything going on—nursing a beer and bullshitting with a couple of guys from high school. Catching Xander's eye, Zane grinned and tipped his beer bottle in greeting.

Xander inclined his head in reply, then faced Quinn again. Zane, too, was a SEAL, but he was based out of Coronado while Xander was in Virginia. For the past ten years, family reunions were few and far between. And while getting a chance to spend some time with Zane—and the rest of their family—was the main reason he'd agreed to attend their class reunion, he was in no hurry to leave Quinn's company.

"Zane doesn't look for trouble, either," Xander said.

"He doesn't have to," she murmured, still looking past him to Zane, definite interest in her gaze. "I bet it finds him anyway."

It did. That was Zane. Always wanting to prove himself, ready and willing to go after whatever he wanted, no holds barred, while Xander was more patient. Content to take things as they came. To wait them out.

Usually. He was usually patient. Usually content to wait things out.

And he was never, ever jealous of his brother.

But he didn't like being looked through—passed over. Not for any man. Especially not for Zane. Not from the girl he still dreamed about.

The one woman he'd always wanted.

He shifted forward, waited until she focused on him, the humor in her eyes—as if she was laughing at him—pricking his ego.

Poking his pride.

Leaning down so he could speak directly into her ear,

he braced one hand on the bar behind her, inches from her arm. Close enough to see her eyes widen slightly, to catch her small, sharp inhale. "I don't look for trouble," he repeated, then eased back and let his gaze drop to that mouth of hers for one long moment before meeting her eyes again. "But I know how to handle it when it comes my way."

QUINN RAISED AN EYEBROW—one of the many, many tricks she'd taught herself over the years—and maintained eye contact with Xander. She even managed a brief grin, just to prove how truly unaffected she was by his nearness. The intensity of his gaze.

There was only one teeny, tiny, irritating problem.

She couldn't breathe.

No, really, it was as if he'd just, *whoosh*, sucked all the air out of the room, and possibly the entire building, with his words, the husky, sexy timbre of his voice.

Men. Can't live with them, can't live without them.

Can't ever, ever let them get the upper hand.

A reminder that gave her the wherewithal to tip her head and give him a slow, thorough once-over, much like he'd given her.

Like all men gave her.

It wasn't a hardship. Xander Bennett had always been easy on the eyes. Supershort brown hair, clean-shaven with a sharp jaw and eyes more gold than brown, he was the poster child for the all-American boy next door.

If you liked that sort of thing.

She didn't. Usually. But on Xander, it worked. It worked really, really well.

It was his nose, she decided. There was a slight bend to it—a bend that hadn't been there in high school. One that suggested it'd been broken.

One that suggested there might just be more to him than meets the eye.

Despite the jeans, crisp button-down shirt and cowboy boots, he looked more soldier—or in his case, she guessed, sailor—than ranch hand out on the town. Tall with broad shoulders, he had a bearing about him that said not only could he handle trouble, easily, but that trouble would be smart to stay away from him in the first place.

Quinn hadn't always been smart.

But those times, they were a-changin'.

"Just make sure any trouble you handle," she said, "doesn't happen at Myer's. I've been warned about you."

He eased back, allowing her to slip around him and go back behind the bar. Once there, with the safety of the wide, scarred wood between them, she took a deep, careful breath.

Better. Much, much better.

"You were warned about me?" he asked.

"We—" she gestured to Steve, the other bartender, then to Lila, the waitress "—were warned about you and your brother." A customer held up his empty glass and she pulled him a fresh beer. "Guess Dianne is holding a grudge over that last ruckus you two caused in here."

"We paid for the damages," Xander said of what Dianne, Quinn's boss and the owner of Myer's, had described as a battle royale two years ago that had taken out four tables, six sets of chairs, three bar stools and the door to the women's restroom, not to mention countless glassware. "And we didn't cause it."

"No? So you were innocent bystanders caught in the fray?"

"More like targets." He lifted a shoulder. "A couple of guys wanted to prove they could take us on."

Quinn exchanged the beer for money and picked up the

customer's empty glass. "And you wanted to prove they couldn't?" She rolled her eyes. "Men. Such fragile egos."

"I don't have to prove anything," he said, the quiet intensity, the way he held her gaze telling her he spoke the truth. "And my ego is just fine."

She bet.

"Yet you fought them anyway," she said.

Another shrug. "Zane needed me."

"Don't tell me, the big, bad rebel turned bigger, badder SEAL couldn't handle himself in a bar fight?"

"He can handle himself. But when that fifth guy jumped in, I thought I'd help even the odds."

She shook her head. "Wait…you and your brother fought five other guys?"

"Something like that," he said, all matter-of-fact, as if being outnumbered was nothing new.

Or anything to be worried about.

"Something like that?" she repeated. "So there were more?"

"You know Zane's a SEAL?" he asked instead of answering—which told her all she needed to know. There'd been more than five other guys.

Seemed when Dianne told the story to her employees, she'd left out the best part.

"I—along with everyone in the city limits—know you both are." Quinn took an order, poured rum into a glass then added cola. "Even all these years later, the Bennett boys are the talk of the town."

The brothers both joined the military—Xander going the officer route through Annapolis, Zane enlisting—out of high school. And though they'd taken different paths, on opposite sides of the country, they'd both become SEALs, real-life American heroes.

"And now," she continued, after handing the rum and

cola to her customer, "you're back for our illustrious ten-year high school reunion, where you and Zane will be honored for your service to our country and doing the old class proud."

"You keeping tabs on us, Quinn?"

Her mouth dried at the sound of him saying her name, which was so crazy—not to mention unacceptable—she patted his hand, like he was an adorable little kid wishing for something far out of his range. "Now, don't be getting delusions of grandeur, sailor." Yes, she used the term instead of his rank to show she saluted to no man. And to get herself back on even ground. "Like I said, everyone knows. This is a small town, remember? Everyone knows everything about everyone."

"That bothers you."

She jerked, her fingers twitching on the back of his knuckles before she curled them into her palm and slid her hand away. Stupid of her to hope he hadn't noticed her reaction. The man saw way more than the average Joe.

Way more than she wanted him to.

His gaze was steady and intense on hers, as if he had all night to stand here, as if he wanted nothing more than to get inside of her head. To figure her out.

She knew better.

Men didn't want inside her head. They wanted in her pants.

As for figuring her out…any curiosity they might have about her, about who she really was, what she wanted, her hopes and dreams and ambitions, fell by the wayside once they accomplished their first goal.

So she let them see only what she wanted them to see.

And told herself she no longer wished for more.

"I'm an open book. A busy one," she said pointedly, grabbing a bottle of the beer his brother was drinking. She opened it and set it in front of Xander. "On the house. A thank-you for your service." When he didn't take it, she slid it even farther toward him. "Enjoy your evening."

Not quite as blatant as if she'd just told him he was dismissed, but pretty close.

He got the not-so-subtle hint and picked up the bottle. Hesitated as if he didn't want to leave. Didn't want to walk away from her.

But he would. They all did eventually.

Which was why she'd learned to do the walking first.

"It was real good seeing you again, Quinn," he said quietly before turning and making his way toward his brother and their high school cronies.

He didn't look back.

And she'd lick a bar stool before admitting to anyone— even herself—how much she'd wanted him to.

Or that it'd been good seeing him, too.

2

"WHEW," LENNY CORWIN said under his breath as he ogled the curvy blonde walking past them. "I'd like to take her for a ride. She's turned me down four times, though. But she's giving you the do-me look, Xander. You gonna go for it?"

At the pool table, Xander gave the blonde a dismissive glance then lined up his next shot. "Zane went out with her."

"So?"

"Bennett brothers don't share," Joe Beck piped up from his spot watching Xander clear the table. Joe sucked at pool. Always had. Xander almost felt bad about taking his money. Almost. "Remember? Any chick one of them does—"

Xander lifted his gaze, spearing the other man with a narrow look.

"Dates," Joe corrected. He cleared his throat. Took a sip of beer. "Any chick one of them dates," he repeated, "is on the other's do-not-touch list."

"Is that why the two of you live on opposite coasts? To keep the field clear for the other?"

Zane laughed. "No. It's so we can spread the joy of the Bennett brothers around. Our little favor to womankind."

At their table in the corner, Kyle Daley poured his fourth glass of beer, emptying the pitcher. "Methinks it's challenge time."

Challenge time.

Jesus Christ.

Xander banked the eight ball into the side pocket. "No."

"C'mon, it's tradition," Mike Harris said.

Kyle leaned back—and almost toppled over before catching his balance. Another thing that hadn't changed. Kyle couldn't hold his beer worth shit.

After two attempts, he lifted his feet—one, then the other—onto the table. "He's got a point. We've been issuing challenges since second grade when Joe dared the two of you to jump off the dugout roof to see who could land closest to the pitcher's mound."

Zane had won, beating Xander by six inches and breaking his ankle in the process.

"Or Mike's cookie challenge. Xander won that one. How many snickerdoodles did you eat? Four dozen?"

Xander's stomach turned. He hasn't been able to eat a snickerdoodle since.

And he loved snickerdoodles.

"Four dozen and two," he corrected. He nodded in his brother's direction. "Zane upchucked at forty-nine."

"Drag racing on Old March Road."

"Who could catch the most bass when we camped at Adobe Creek."

"Who could get the most applause singing 'Living on a Prayer' in the cafeteria."

Xander caught Zane's eye roll, amusement on his brother's face. The challenges hadn't been so bad when they'd been young.

But he didn't play games now.

And his career gave him plenty of challenges. He didn't need these bozos coming up with stupid dares so he could prove himself.

Xander shot the last ball into the pocket and Zane stood. "I think we've outgrown being dumbasses."

Mike looked like a kid whose favorite toy just got run over by a semi. "We can't have a reunion without a challenge."

Joe rejoined them, carrying a full pitcher of beer. "And I've got the perfect one. Remember the girl everyone wanted to date in school?"

Zane frowned. "No."

Of course Zane didn't know who Joe was talking about. Back in high school, if Zane wanted to date a girl, he dated her.

He'd always been the master at getting what he wanted.

But Xander... He glanced at the woman behind the bar, doling out drinks and sexy smiles.

Yeah. He remembered.

"You mean the Princess?" Zane asked, but he wasn't looking at Quinn. He was watching Xander.

Shit. He'd given himself away.

"Yep, the Princess. Quinn Oswald was the finest girl in our class. Nobody here scored with her then and nobody's scored with her since she moved back to Little Creek."

From his tone, good ol' Joe had given it his best shot.

The bastard.

Xander's fingers tightened on the pool stick and Zane put a hand on his arm. They'd always had the whole twin sixth sense thing going on, could always tell when the other was hurt or in trouble.

Or slowly getting so pissed off, they wanted to wrap a pool stick around an old friend's neck.

"We don't bet on sex," Zane said, speaking for them both.

Xander didn't mind. They were twins, not clones, with their own individual sets of strengths and weaknesses. But there was one very important thing they had in common.

They had each other's backs.

Always.

"Not sex." But Joe's disappointed tone said that was exactly what he'd meant. "A date. Just a date."

Kyle grinned. "To the reunion dance. Last night of the event, everyone's wearing clothes. Nothing rude about that, right? It'll be like prom night all over again."

"A date with Quinn Oswald to the reunion dance. Let's make it easy on her and keep the choice between the two of you," Mike said to Xander and Zane. "Challenge issued."

Xander met Zane's eyes. Son of a bitch. His brother was seriously contemplating accepting this stupid dare.

Zane never could turn down a challenge. And it wasn't about proving himself. It was about one thing and one thing only.

Winning.

"Yeah, sure," Zane said with a shrug. "It's better than raw eggs. And should be more fun."

Xander glanced at Quinn again. If he didn't accept, the challenge would still go on. Zane would pursue Quinn with the same single-minded focus he used to get whatever he wanted.

Except he didn't want Quinn. Not really.

But Xander did.

And he'd be damned if he'd spend the next two weeks sitting on his ass while his brother got the girl.

It was time he went after what he wanted.

He nodded at Zane. "I'm in."

Ah, QUINN THOUGHT as she carried cleaning supplies down the short hall. *Finally.* The best part of the night and her absolute favorite part of her job.

Closing time.

She stepped into the bar, set her supplies down then pulled her hair back into a short ponytail. A Norah Jones song played over the radio, Norah singing about love and loss, the melody mellow and heartbreaking.

Shutting her eyes, Quinn inhaled deeply. God, she used to love this song. Had danced to it just after being named homecoming queen.

It'd been her shining moment and, at the time, everything she'd ever wanted. Wearing a sparkly blue dress, that plastic crown on top of her head, had been the pinnacle of her high school career. While Nora crooned over the gym's loud speakers, she'd swayed in the arms of her king while the entire student body watched.

Their princess had become their queen.

Her eyes opened.

Princess. She snorted and sprayed cleaner over the bar. More like Cinderella now. A fairy tale in reverse.

If they could only see me now, she thought, scrubbing the ancient wood with enough force to wear a hole clean through it.

How the mighty Quinn had fallen.

Oh, that was right. They could see her and they did, each and every day. And she'd made it so easy for them, slinking back to Little Creek after her divorce, desperate to get back on her feet.

Determined to make it on her own.

Broke but not broken.

Not completely. Just...changed.

She was smarter. Stronger. And she still had her pride.

It didn't do much to keep her warm at night but it did help her face each day with her head held high.

Humming along to the end of the song, she walked out from behind the bar with a tray and began clearing tables.

The song ended, and in that brief few seconds before the next one started, the nape of her neck prickled. Frowning, she rubbed it, trying to shake off the sensation that something was…well, not wrong, exactly…just off.

She stepped farther into the room and peeked around the partition into the alcove.

And met Xander Bennett's eyes.

Oh, yeah, something was definitely off because desire swept through her, hard and fast, almost knocking her back a step. Her heart raced. Her head spun. Her stomach dropped. It was like she was in a full-on swoon.

It was exhilarating and exciting and terrifying all at once.

It was also dangerous. Deceptive. A girl could be lured into believing she could play with fire and not get burned. Or worse, that the pain of touching the flame would be worth it in the end.

Lies. Vicious, hurtful lies.

"What are you doing?" she asked, unable to hide her irritation. Why should she try? It was late, she was tired and he was ticking her off. He wasn't supposed to be here.

She wasn't supposed to find him attractive in more than a passing "isn't he pretty to look at" way. There should be no racing, spinning or dropping.

And absolutely no swooning.

"Waiting for you," he said.

Damn it. And there shouldn't be any sort of thrill from three simple words.

"Didn't Steve tell you it's closing time? *Was* closing time," she corrected, checking her watch. "Twenty minutes ago."

Xander nodded. "He told me."

She hesitated, but that seemed to be all he had to say on the subject. A man of few words.

It was intriguing, how he didn't blab on and on. How he thought through his answers, spoke slowly and carefully. Intriguing and more appealing than she liked to admit.

Most guys talked and talked and talked—mainly about themselves. Trying so hard to impress her. To get her to spend more time with them. To get her into bed. Or else they talked about her—more specifically, they talked about how beautiful she was, her eyes as blue as the sky, her hair like silk…blah, blah, blah.

If she wanted a description of what she looked like, she'd check out her reflection in the mirror.

"Steve told you it was closing time," she repeated, "and yet, you're still here." She narrowed her eyes. "He didn't tell you to leave?"

Another nod. "I told him I was staying." He shrugged as if he had no idea what the problem was. "He seemed okay with it."

"Of course he was okay with it," she said with an eye roll. "You're a freaking SEAL. He was probably terrified you'd eviscerate him with a stir straw."

One side of his mouth hitched up in a boyish grin. No way she'd ever admit how adorable she found it. "I'm not sure that's possible," he said. "Maybe two stir straws. And one of those plastic swords. They seem pretty pointy."

She swallowed a smile. Seriously? Good-looking, an American hero and funny?

She glanced at the heavens. Someone up there had a wicked and perverse sense of humor.

"Well, Steve may have been fine with letting you stick around," she said, "but I'm not. You know what they say. You don't have to go home. But you can't stay here. You and your brother and your buddies can always come back later for another Let's Reminisce About Our High School Glory Days meeting. We reopen at 3:00 p.m."

He headed toward her, his walk deceptively lazy. "It wasn't."

She frowned. The man was really messing with her head if she couldn't follow a simple conversation.

A simple conversation in which she was doing most of the talking. "It wasn't what?" she asked.

He came closer, his gaze on her like a touch, one she felt to her bones. She ducked her head, pretended to focus on loading dirty glasses onto her tray. Hey, she was only human, made of flesh and blood and, it seemed, an abundance of hormones, and it was disconcerting having that much focus on her.

She felt exposed, like he was looking past her face and body, trying to see inside her head.

She shook that fanciful notion off. He wasn't interested in her thoughts and feelings. No man was.

He stopped at the opposite side of the table. "High school wasn't my glory days."

No, she supposed it wasn't. From what she could remember, he'd been popular enough in school. Not on par with the more outgoing Zane, but Xander had been well liked, smart and an accomplished athlete.

Now he had a successful career as a SEAL and, if she had to guess, plans for his future that didn't include returning to Little Creek with no money, no job prospects or viable employment skills and no idea what he was going to do with his life. His future was probably all mapped out, complete with goals he accomplished with regularity.

Only brighter days were ahead for him. Brighter days.

"Lucky you," she said drily, resentment dripping into her tone, "not to have peaked in high school."

"That what you think?" he asked quietly, his gaze too knowing. "That you peaked in high school?"

She wasn't sure, and that was the problem. "What I

think is that I have a lot of work left to do. And you're keeping me from it."

"I'll help."

She set a glass on the tray with a sharp crack. "I don't want or need your help."

"You shouldn't be here by yourself. I'll wait until you're done then walk you to your car."

His concern for her was sweet but she couldn't trust it. Couldn't believe it was real.

No matter how much she found herself wanting to.

"I'm perfectly safe," she said, sashaying around the table to stand before him. "Besides, we both know what you want—and it's not to see me safely to my car. And while I'm flattered…" Flattered. Incredibly tempted. Why quibble? "I'm not interested in hooking up with an old high school classmate."

A horrible lie, as she was becoming more interested by the moment, especially standing this close to him. But she couldn't let him know it so she gave him a light, condescending pat on his cheek. "Don't worry. I'm sure there will be plenty of women at the reunion eager to take a trip down memory lane with you."

Something in his eyes changed, lit with challenge and she froze, her fingertips on his cheek.

Damn it, she'd gone too far.

Before she could pull away, he caught her wrist, held it lightly. Then tugged her closer, the move so slow, she knew he was giving her a chance to break free should she want to, that at her slightest resistance, he'd let go.

But if she backed down, he might get the crazy idea that she was afraid of him. And that was unacceptable.

She expected him to pull her against him, told herself she wasn't disappointed when he left inches between their bodies.

Used all her willpower not to close that distance between them herself.

"You shouldn't be alone, Quinn," he said, his low voice doing odd things to her stomach. The way he said her name messing with her mind.

His words causing her throat to tighten.

She chose to be alone. It was smarter, safer than counting on someone to be there for her.

But it was also lonely as hell.

And, oh, how it grated to admit that.

She stepped back and he dropped her wrist. "Actually," she said, proud of her even tone, "I prefer being alone."

Heart racing, skin tingling from his touch, she nonetheless managed to hold his gaze steadily.

After several long, agonizing moments, he finally nodded.

And walked away.

Just like she knew he would.

3

OVER AN HOUR LATER, Quinn locked Myer's front door, tugged on it once, then turned and headed down the street.

"Where the hell is your car?"

She whirled around, her hand already digging into her purse for pepper spray. When she saw who it was, she considered giving him a good dose of the stuff anyway on principle alone.

"Xander! God. What is wrong with you? You don't just…" She waved her hand like a lunatic, which made sense as she was feeling extremely off-kilter. "Jump out at a woman on a dark street. What are you, a psycho? Where did you even come from?" The street had been empty a moment ago, she was sure of it. "Don't tell me, temporary civilian life is too boring for you, so you decided to do a little nighttime rappelling down the side of the bakery so you could scare the crap out of me."

"Your car," he ground out, shoulders rigid, expression set. "Where is it?"

She raised her eyebrows. "What's your problem? I'm the one who just had a heart attack."

"I waited to make sure you got to your car safely." He

stabbed a thumb in the direction of the empty parking lot. "Where is it?"

Giddiness bubbled up in her chest. He'd waited for her? To make sure she was okay? She'd never had a man wait for her before.

It was sweet.

And had her attitude softening toward him.

"My car is at a used lot in Albuquerque," she said. "At least, I'm guessing it's still there. Not many people have much use for a ten-year-old compact with one hundred and fifty thousand miles. I sure didn't."

He shook his head. "You don't have a car."

"Nope."

"You don't have a car," he repeated, making her wonder if he'd suffered a recent brain injury affecting his short-term memory. "You walk home."

It wasn't a question, more like a statement of disbelief, but she answered him anyway. "Yes."

He stared at her as if she'd just told him she flew to the moon every night. His mouth barely moved when he spoke—how did he do that? Was he a part-time ventriloquist?

And then his words penetrated her brain.

"Are you stupid?"

Her eyes narrowed. That little giddy bubble in her chest popped with a sharp poke of reality and any softening went stone-cold hard.

"Not even a little," she said. "But you must be."

Turning on her heel, she walked away, worrying that Xander was right. She was stupid.

Because for a second there, she'd wanted him to be different.

"SHIT," XANDER MUTTERED as Quinn stalked away, all long legs and pissed-off attitude.

He caught up with her in two strides. She sped up, her hand in her front pocket, the sound of the heels of her boots clicking on the sidewalk echoing in the night. She couldn't outrun him, which only increased his initial irritation.

She couldn't outrun an attacker.

"What's in your purse?" he asked.

"Seriously? First you wait in the dark for me like a stalker and now you're mugging me?" She tsked. Twice. "Your mother must be so disappointed."

"When I first approached you—"

"Scared the crap out of me," she corrected.

He ignored it. If she'd been more aware of her surroundings, he wouldn't have startled her. Not that he was going to mention that.

He'd been enough of an idiot already. He didn't need to add to it.

"You went for something in your purse," he continued. "And as disappointed as my mom would be in me, she'd hate for me to come home with a bullet wound and bleed on her floors. Especially if she finds out I didn't even get my apology out first."

Quinn gave an eye roll so huge, he was surprised she didn't lose her equilibrium and tip over. "It's not a gun. It's pepper spray. So no blood, just a few tears. Which might help make your apology—" she said *apology* as if she'd put air quotes around it "—seem sincere."

"I deserve that," he said, "but I don't say anything I don't mean."

She slid him a "that's bullshit" look.

He'd have to prove it to her.

Except she was still walking, going at that fast clip, her shoulders rigid, chin lifted. His window of opportunity for getting her to listen to him, to believe him, was being slammed shut.

On his head.

"I shouldn't have said you were stupid."

She ignored him.

"Quinn." He touched her arm and she stopped. Stared straight ahead. "I'm sorry." He stepped around her, ducked his head so he could meet her eyes. "I'm sorry," he repeated, knowing damn well anything worth doing, worth saying, was worth putting in 100 percent effort. "I know you're not stupid."

Tipping her head to the side, she eyed him with no little amount of mistrust. "How?"

He frowned, tried to concentrate on the mission at hand but it was tough as hell when all he could think about was pressing his mouth to the curve of her neck. Breathing in her scent. Tasting her skin. "What?"

"How do you know I'm not stupid? You don't even really know me. We went to high school together but we weren't friends. We didn't even hang out with the same crowd."

She waited but he was struggling with what to tell her, what to say that didn't make him sound like some pathetic loser who'd been hung up on her ten years ago.

Or worse, who was still hung up on her.

She frowned, but in her eyes he didn't see disdain so much as…disappointment. "So much for 'I don't say anything I don't mean.'"

And she walked away from him.

Again.

It was becoming a habit. He couldn't say he liked it much.

He cleared his throat and prepared to out himself. Sometimes being honorable, always doing the right thing, was a pain in the ass.

"English class."

She jerked to a stop and whirled around. "What?"

"Our senior year. We were in the same Advanced Placement English class..."

And he could tell by her frown that she didn't remember.

Yeah, his ego was taking a hell of a beating tonight.

"And you had the highest grade," he continued.

She took a step toward him this time.

Progress.

"You remembered that?" she asked.

When it came to her, he remembered everything. How she played with her hair when she was reading, twisting a strand of it around her finger, oblivious to everything going on near her. Her husky laugh that turned everyone's heads. How her face would light up when she debated with the teacher over a book's theme.

But he'd already given away too much. Just waiting for her to finish work exposed his true intentions, but when he'd seen Zane talking with her at the bar after they'd accepted that stupid challenge, he'd known he had to step up his game if he wanted to win.

If he wanted Quinn.

"I know you're not stupid," he told her, "because you carry pepper spray and you're not afraid to use it. Because you left the bar out the front door and not the back, which leads to an alley, and because you've got your cell phone in your hand—" He nodded at the hand she still had in her pocket. "Ready to call for help should you feel threatened." He stepped closer, relieved and grateful when she didn't back away. "You're not stupid," he murmured, "but you are taking a risk, walking home alone at night."

"It's a safe town. Half the people here don't even lock their doors at night."

"Bad things happen in every town. No matter how small or safe." He'd seen too much ugliness in the world to pretend there were areas it didn't exist. Couldn't let her go if it meant the possibility of her getting hurt. "I'll walk you home."

"Hang out in the middle of the night with a man I barely know, one who knows a thousand ways to kill someone? That seems riskier than me going it alone."

She was messing with him. Pushing him. And it was late enough, and he was tired enough, to want to push back, just a little. He edged even closer, so close she had to tip her head back to maintain eye contact. But she held her ground. Her scent, something soft with a hint of spice, wrapped around him in the warm, still night.

"You're safe with me."

Her sharp, sardonic grin was at odds with the wariness in her eyes. "I'm not so sure about that."

He stilled. "Are you afraid of me, Quinn?"

"No, just smart enough not to accept every offer I get from some good-looking sailor in town for a few days."

"I only want to walk you home."

She laughed softly, the light sound almost his undoing. "You sure about that?"

The quiet words blew through him and he couldn't help it. He grinned, slow and easy and, holding her gaze, told her the truth. "No, that's not all I want. But it's what I'll settle for. Let me walk you home, Quinn."

Damn him. Damn him!

It wasn't his promise that had Quinn's stomach quivering with a mix of lust and nerves. It wasn't his honesty in admitting to wanting more from her than a 3:00 a.m., one-mile stroll through their hometown.

That had her seriously considering taking him up on his offer.

It was his self-deprecating smile.

Why did he have to have a sense of humor? Or at least, a sense of the absurd.

It was her weakness.

One of them, anyway. She seemed to have more than her fair share when it came to men.

Especially ones who looked as good as Xander.

"Uh-huh," she said, crossing her arms and willing herself to stay strong in the face of…well…in the face of all six feet plus of broad-shouldered, clean-cut handsomeness. "And why should I believe you?"

He watched her in a way that made her antsy. Made her want to curl into herself and hide from his view. "Why shouldn't you?"

Good point. She had no reason to think he was being anything less than 100 percent truthful.

Then again, she had no reason to trust him, either.

And that was what he was asking for. Her trust.

Easy to ask for. Harder—much, much harder—to give.

"Nothing is going to happen that you don't want to happen," he said when she remained silent. "I promise."

She had to give him credit. He was excellent at the whole "I'm one of the good guys" routine. She wanted to believe him.

And really, what would it hurt? Yes, he made her nervous, but not in a "he's going to murder me and hide my body in his mom's basement" way.

More like a basic, elemental, sexual way.

He made her want. Made her remember how long it had been since a man had touched her. Had kissed her. How long it had been since a man had moved inside her.

Her mouth dried. Her pelvis contracted with need.

Yeah, he made her want.

Damn him again.

It soothed her nerves to at least know she wasn't in this alone. He wanted her, as well. Hadn't he practically admitted that just a moment ago?

She wasn't sure if that made this whole situation better. Or worse.

But it definitely made it more interesting.

"My apartment's on Brookside Court," she said. That was over a mile away in the opposite direction of his mother's house. Which meant he'd have to walk back here to get his truck. "Still want to walk me home?"

"Absolutely."

She shrugged and told herself she was not thrilled at the way he didn't even hesitate. "Well, then, it looks like you've found yourself a damsel in no distress. Let's go."

He fell into step beside her, big and broad and silent and, she hated to admit, comforting.

It was nice not being alone.

So nice a girl could get used to it if she wasn't careful.

"You're not staying with your mom?" he asked as they turned left onto First Street.

The house she'd grown up in was on Harrison Road, outside of town. "Mom moved to Seattle four years ago."

She felt him glance at her. "But you came back to Little Creek. After your divorce."

She wasn't surprised he knew she'd been married. That she'd failed at it. Like she'd told him, everyone in Little Creek knew everything about everyone else.

"Yeah, I came back. Desperate times and all that," she said, injecting a note of lightness she didn't feel into her tone. "Mom invited me to move in with her at her new place, but she has a boyfriend now and I felt I was in the way. Plus, I guess I wanted something familiar, and Little Creek sure fit that bill."

It was safe. A place she could recuperate and lick her wounds and figure out what to do next.

"You didn't want to stay in Albuquerque?"

"Phoenix," she corrected. "Albuquerque was just the place my car died on the drive back here. And, no, I didn't want to stay."

Living in Little Creek might bring daily reminders of who she used to be, but staying in Phoenix would have been worse.

There she was reminded of the person she'd become. Of what she'd almost been willing to sacrifice to hold on to a man who wasn't worthy of her.

Xander was doing that whole watchful thing again, waiting for her to go on. Maybe it was the night, the dark surrounding them, the feeling as if they were the only two people in the world, or maybe it was because it was so late and she was tired.

Or maybe it was because Xander was listening—really listening. That he was interested in what she had to say.

Maybe it was because, for some reason she refused to delve into too deeply, she wanted to tell him. Wanted him to know something about her, something no one else did.

His fault for bringing up English class. For remembering her in that class all those years ago.

For remembering something about herself she could be proud of.

"Phoenix was Peter's town," she heard herself say. "My ex. He was raised there, has family there and I realized that *our* friends were really *his* friends. Once I left him, there was nothing there for me, so I came home."

It was the hardest thing she'd ever done. Harder even,

than finally going through with her threats and divorcing Peter.

The bastard.

"I'm sorry," Xander said, "that things didn't work out."

She laughed but the sound held no humor. "Yeah, well, that's what happens when you marry someone who lies and cheats. Things don't work out."

Xander stiffened beside her. "He cheated on you?"

Her face warmed but at least it was dark enough he couldn't see her blush. "It doesn't matter now. I left him."

She'd left him, but it had taken her finding out about his third affair to finally do that. She'd been so desperate to hold on to her marriage. Wanted so badly to believe that he could change.

Wanted him to love her enough to change for her.

Lesson learned. People were who they were and no amount of wishing and hoping could make them different.

She picked up her pace, the confession of her marriage, of what really happened, spurring her to move faster, to get home sooner.

To get away from Xander.

He kept up easily—no surprise, the man was a highly trained SEAL for God's sake. Did she really think she could outwalk him?

They fell silent, and when she spotted the light on at her apartment door, she breathed a sigh of relief. Dug her key out of her purse. "This is me," she said, heading up the stone steps, surprised when he followed.

With a shrug, she let him. Unlocked her door and made the mistake of turning to say goodbye. To thank him.

He stood on the step below, leaving them eye to eye. Mouth to mouth. In the soft glow of the light, his eyes were dark and he smelled really, really good.

She swallowed. "Thanks for the escort."

He nodded. Turned only to face her again. "Peter is an idiot."

"No argument there," she said, but was surprised by the vehemence in his tone, the utter belief. "Although I'm not sure you're the best to judge seeing as how you've never met him."

"He let you go," he said simply. "That's all I need to know."

Her scalp prickled. Her palms went damp. Why did he have to say that? Why did he have to look at her that way, as if she was something precious? Something worth holding on to?

She could have resisted him, she assured herself. Could have sent him on his way with a smile and "see you later," but now?

Now she couldn't let him go.

"What if I want it to happen?" she asked.

"What?"

She licked her lips. Swallowed. *In for a penny*, she thought...

"You said that nothing was going to happen that I didn't want to happen." Inhaling deeply, she did something she hadn't done in a long, long time. She took a chance. "What if I want it to happen?"

$$4$$

QUINN'S PULSE POUNDED in her ears, her words echoing in her head.

What if I want it to happen?

Being brave was not for the faint of heart. She wondered how Xander did it on a daily basis.

Because while he stood there, still as a statue, cool, calm and collected, she was a heart-racing, palms-sweating, stomach-turning mess. She didn't make the first move with men. She didn't have to.

A fact she should be incredibly grateful for. Putting herself out there like this sucked. It made her vulnerable, too dependent on what a man wanted. Gave him all the control.

And she'd promised herself she'd never, ever let a man have that much power over her again.

"What do you want to happen?" he asked, his gaze searching. Seeking. Looking for the truth.

But she couldn't give him that. Couldn't open herself up to him. Not that much.

"You walked me home," she said, unable to answer his question. "Right to my door. You waited for me," she continued accusingly.

If he hadn't waited, if he hadn't walked her home, she

wouldn't be here, out on her stoop in the middle of the night, stuttering and stammering and wishing she had enough courage to go after what she wanted.

This was his fault. All his fault for being so stubborn and steady and way, way too tempting. For making her believe in the notion of being taken care of. Of being cared for.

Those kind of crazy thoughts had gotten her into too much trouble in her life. She'd spent years fantasizing about the unattainable, things like having a true partner, a man she could count on. Who wanted her for herself and not just her looks. Who'd be there for her always.

Who wouldn't walk away.

Fantasies, she scoffed to herself. Stupid fairy tales little kids believed in. What she used to believe in. What she used to crave. A white knight swooping in to save her.

To love her.

She'd grown up.

"What do you want, Quinn?" he asked, his husky tone reverberating in her chest. In her core. "Tell me and it's yours."

See? He made her believe him. As if all she had to do was ask and he'd snag the very stars from the sky, give her the world.

Oh, he was a dangerous, dangerous man.

"I want to appease my curiosity," she said, edging closer so that her thighs brushed his. He stiffened and while his expression didn't change, she heard the small catch of his breath. Rode the thrill that gave her and slid her hands up his wide, solid chest, before linking them behind his neck. She held his gaze. "Don't you?"

His hands circled her wrists but he didn't tug her away. "You don't owe me anything."

She couldn't help it. She smiled. "You're right. I don't owe you anything. This isn't payback for the escort home."

"Then what is it?"

Good question.

One she wasn't sure she wanted to know the answer to. His fault again for making that silent strength of his so appealing. For wanting to protect her.

For making her want things, want him, with a force that stole her breath.

"It's either the worst idea I've had in a long time," she told him, giving him as much as honesty as she could, "or the best."

"It's not the worst."

She raised an eyebrow. "No? Then what are we waiting for?"

What was *he* waiting for? She'd made the first move—and the second and third. She'd be damned if she'd make the final one.

If she did, she'd always wonder, always worry that maybe, just maybe, despite the heat in his eyes, the way he looked at her, she was in this alone.

And that was unacceptable.

Because she was afraid it might just break her heart.

She could practically see his brain working. Analyzing. Going through a list of pros and cons. She had no idea why she found it so attractive while she waited with the proverbial baited breath.

This was all part of the game men and women played—push and pull then push again—and while she'd sat the bench for a long time, had taken herself out of the rotation, she knew what to do when she stepped up to the plate.

She pressed against him—thighs, pelvis, belly and chest. Desire flared in his eyes, his fingers tightened on her wrists, but he didn't pull her closer.

Didn't give her what she yearned for.

He had control, she'd give him that, and she suddenly, viciously, wanted to test that control.

Wanted to be the woman to make him lose it.

"What do you want, Xander?" she whispered, repeating his earlier question to her. "Tell me and it's yours."

He groaned and slid his hands down her arms to her elbows. Pulled her even closer by slow degrees. Her breasts grew heavy; her nipples tightened. And just when she was on the precipice of giving up, of giving into the pressure building inside her and making the move that would finally, finally bring their mouths together, he lowered his head and kissed her.

It was a soft kiss, barely the brush of his lips against hers. Then another soft kiss before he settled his mouth on hers, the move slow and easy and so gentle it made her heart trip. A far cry from what she wanted. She needed the heat and flash of desire, craved the sharp burn of lust, not this tender, almost sweet seduction that slowed her senses, drugged her mind.

That made her risk forgetting all her hard-earned lessons about protecting her heart.

No, no, she wouldn't forget. Wouldn't give him the upper hand just because he kissed like a freaking dream and felt like a fantasy come to life. This wasn't about sweetness or gentleness. This attraction between them might not be purely physical, but she sure as hell planned on pretending it was.

If only for her own peace of mind.

Stabbing her fingers into his short hair, she angled her head to deepen the kiss and touched the tip of her tongue against the seam of his lips. A shudder ran through him, and a moan rose in his throat, echoed in hers as he took over the kiss, sliding his tongue into her mouth, his hands gripping her hips.

Better, much, much better.

He kissed her with a hunger that only increased her own, his fingers curved over her ass, his thumbs against her hip bones. She scraped her fingernails lightly against his scalp, and with a low growl, he lifted her off her feet, took the two steps needed to reach her front door and pressed her against it.

Desire dug in deep, had her rolling her hips against his arousal, and he went off like a rocket, his kiss turning feral, his hands skimming her curves, sliding up her sides, his fingers brushing against the slopes of her breasts.

This was what she needed. The feel of him, strong and solid against her, his mouth on hers, rough and wild. But it wasn't enough. Wasn't nearly enough to ease the ache between her legs. She needed him there, hot and hard and filling her. Wanted his mouth on her breasts, tugging and sucking the straining peaks. Wanted to wrap her legs around him and let him take her here and now, against her front door with the starlit sky overhead, the quiet and dark surrounding them.

She ached to be reckless and impulsive and listen to her body and to hell with the consequences. But she'd already made too many mistakes. Had gotten herself into too many messes. She'd come too far to be careless now.

She pushed lightly against his shoulders and he immediately let go. They stared at each other, their chests rising and falling with their rapid breaths. His mouth was a grim line, his shirt wrinkled at the shoulders from where she'd clutched him, trying to get even closer, his hair mussed on the sides, the short strands sticking out.

The taste of him clung to her lips and she licked them, trying to capture it, to hold on to it. His gaze narrowed and he lifted his hand, only to curl his fingers into his palm before tucking both hands behind his back. As if he didn't trust himself not to reach for her. Not to touch her.

She shut her eyes. Exhaled an unsteady breath. Her resolve, already shaky at best, weakened and she knew, if he asked her to, she'd invite him in.

If she did, they could spend the next few hours exploring each other's bodies. Satiating the hunger between them. But what if it didn't? What if, instead of slacking their desire, it only increased it?

What if it made her crave him even more?

She opened her eyes. It was a risk she was willing to take. But only if he initiated it. Only if he asked.

Only if he made the choice she was too afraid to make.

A muscle jumped in his jaw, as if he was grinding his teeth and he swore, viciously, under his breath.

And took a step back.

"I'll wait until you get inside," he said with a nod toward her door, his voice low and gravely. "Don't forget to lock up."

She took it as a sign, a clear one. She'd been granted a reprieve. Fumbling with the key in the lock before remembering she'd already unlocked it, she pushed the door open, dashed inside and slammed it shut. Locked it.

Before she changed her mind.

HE WAS AN IDIOT.

No two ways about it, Xander thought the next morning as he and Zane circled each other in their mother's backyard. He was a grade-A, class-one goddamn idiot. He could have had her. He could have spent the night with Quinn Oswald. Could have fulfilled one or two of those fantasies he'd harbored of her during his teen years.

Not to mention a few he still had swirling around his brain.

He could add taking her against the front door of her apartment to that growing list.

And damned if she wouldn't have let him.

She'd wanted him. He'd seen it in her eyes. He knew the signs and she'd given him every last one. The way she'd kissed him, how she'd touched him. How she'd shifted her hips against him.

But she hadn't been sure. Not 100 percent.

He'd had no choice but to walk away.

Because when he got Quinn into bed—or against a door or on the floor or, hell, in the back of his pickup—he wanted her to be certain. No doubts. No recriminations. No claiming it was a trick of the night or the rush of desire.

He wanted her to choose him.

Until then, he was beating himself up over a lost opportunity.

The punch caught him on the left temple. His head snapped back. His ears rung.

He glared at Zane. Shook his head to clear it. Zane always did have a hell of a right hook.

No use beating himself up when his brother was doing a good job of it for him.

"Kicking your ass isn't nearly as much fun when you're only giving fifty percent," Zane said, dancing out of Xander's reach, taped hands up, weight on the balls of his feet. "Maybe I should go down to the gym. See if there's anyone there who can give me a challenge."

He knew better than to let Zane's trash talk bug him, but he was too wound up from that kiss with Quinn. And, as much as he hated to admit it, too worried about Zane trying to win the challenge.

Xander rolled his shoulders back. Tipped his head side to side and muttered, "Fifty percent my ass."

And he proved it by feigning a grab with his right hand only to crouch low and sweep Zane's legs out from under him.

His brother rolled with it and came up grinning. "Better."

Zane went low, wrapping his arms around Xander's waist, trying to take him down. Something Xander had learned early not to let happen.

Once Zane had you down, you were done.

They'd fought each other their entire lives it seemed, wrestling and boxing and a few times pissed-off grudge matches. They knew each other's strengths as well as weaknesses and, all too often, they ended up in a draw.

But it wasn't for lack of trying on either of their parts.

Xander brought his elbow down hard on Zane's back. Zane grunted and sent two sharp jabs to his side, just under his ribs. Xander took the blows, breathed through the pain then twisted out of Zane's hold. Danced back a few steps. They eyed each other.

Xander narrowed his gaze. Zane looked happy. Too happy.

Shit.

"You took off early last night," he said, avoiding Zane's reach.

"Places to go," Zane said, bobbing and weaving. He winked. "Women to do."

Xander stiffened. He knew Zane didn't mean Quinn. He hadn't even been with her last night, had left the bar well before closing.

Xander had been the one to walk her home. To kiss her. He'd been the one who'd blown his opportunity.

"Any particular woman in mind?" he couldn't help but ask.

Zane hesitated—so unusual for him that Xander pounced, shooting out a right hook. Payback was a bitch. Then he gave Zane's red left cheek a love tap, just to add insult to injury.

Literally.

"Whoever it is," Xander said, forcing his tone to stay mild, "she's got you all twisted."

And if Zane said it was Quinn, Xander might have to kick his ass for real.

"No woman twists me up, brother. You know my motto. No ties. No lies. Though I don't mind if one wants to tie me up. My safe word is *pumpernickel*."

"Nope," Xander said. "Don't need to know that. Though if you did have a woman in mind," he continued, keeping his voice casual, his expression clear, "we can call off the challenge."

Something flashed in Zane's eyes and Xander narrowed his gaze. Holy shit. Was Zane really hung up on someone?

But then Zane shook his head, amped up his grin to smirk. "You bowing out? Because you know the rules. Even if one of us declines to accept a challenge—or quits midway—the other still has to follow through."

Christ, who'd made those rules? A bunch of eight-year-olds?

He snorted softly. Yeah. That was pretty much exactly how old they'd been.

Xander dodged left as they continued to circle one another. "What if we don't?"

"What?"

"What if we don't follow through?" Xander asked with a shrug. "What are they doing to do?"

"Doesn't matter. Our pride's on the line. Pride," he continued, "and my win streak."

Xander straightened. "Bullshit. You lost the last—"

Too late he realized it had been part of a distraction technique because Zane leaped and about knocked Xander on his ass. He caught his balance.

It was on.

They grappled for a good ten minutes, the morning sun beating down on them, their grunts and the sound of landed punches filling the air. Just when Xander thought he had an opening to finish his brother, Zane twisted and turned and slid behind Xander, putting him in a chokehold.

Zane always had been a slippery, sneaky bastard.

"Give?" Zane asked, applying enough pressure to Xander's windpipe to make things interesting.

And for Xander to have absolutely no remorse for slamming his foot down on Zane's instep and then ramming his elbow into his stomach.

Letting go of Xander, Zane bent over. "Mother—"

"Don't even think about it."

They both looked up at the stern female warning to find Kerri, their very pregnant older sister, staring at them from the covered patio, one hand on her hip, the other holding a plate piled high with French toast.

"Hey, sis," Zane said to Kerri, but it came out breathless.

Good. Xander was still trying to catch his own breath.

"You two are like a couple of animals," Kerri said, jabbing a forkful of syrup-drenched French toast their way before shoveling it into her mouth. "You know that, right?" she asked around her mouthful. "What kind of example are you setting for the boys?"

She gestured to the edge of the patio where her sons, four-year-old Joel and two-year-old Teddy watched wide-eyed.

"A bad one," Zane said immediately, but then he sent a thoughtful glance at their nephews. "Though they look like they'd be pretty good sparring partners. What do you think?" he asked Xander as he headed toward the boys. "The bigger one looks pretty tough."

Following his brother's train of thought, Xander edged to the side. "I think I could take the little one."

The boys, having figured out what was about to happen, started squealing with glee. Joel took off but Zane caught him easily, flipped him upside down and tickled him. "Yeah. This one's scrappy. I might need some help."

"I've got my hands full," Xander said, dodging left slowly enough that a giggling Teddy could evade, only to swipe the kid up when he tried to dash to the side. "This one's slippery," he said, pretending to drop Teddy. "Whoops."

"Idiots," Kerri muttered and scooped up another forkful.

"Should you be eating that?" Xander asked.

Kerri froze, the fork still in her mouth. Even the boys went silent.

Zane whistled softly and stepped back, away from Xander, as if putting as much distance between them as possible. "I think you look gorgeous," Zane said. "You're glowing."

Xander shot him a glare as Teddy held his hands and climbed up his legs like a spider monkey. "What?" Xander asked Zane then turned back to Kerri. "What? You're the one who was bawling about gaining too much weight with this pregnancy the last time I called you."

She advanced toward him slowly. "I will kill you," she promised, and he was pretty sure he saw fire shooting from her eyes.

Even at what looked to be fifteen months pregnant, she still managed to scare the shit out of him.

"She means it," Joel said. Still hanging upside down, he twisted and turned like a landed trout. "Daddy says she's got too many hormones."

Teddy, now on Xander's hip, nodded. Looked into Xander's eyes. "Run."

Never let it be said he wasn't smart enough to know the importance of a well-timed retreat.

Especially when it was a battle he had no chance of winning.

So with his nephew clinging to him and his brother on his heels, Xander did the only thing a man in his position could do.

He ran like hell.

5

SOMEONE KNOCKED ON the door.

Sitting at her kitchen table, a textbook open to her left, a notebook to her right and her laptop dead center, Quinn lifted her head and frowned.

She'd been back in Little Creek for just over a year and could count on one hand the number of visitors she'd had during that time.

And that included the mailman and the lady who'd fixed the toilet a few months back.

Now, in the span of—she checked her phone—an hour and a half, she was on her second unexpected guest of the day.

Guess she was enjoying a resurgence of her old high school popularity.

Hooray.

Whoever it was knocked again, and she stood with a sigh then crossed her tiny kitchen into the equally small living room and opened the door.

Well, well, well. What did she have here?

Okay, she knew what she had. She had Xander Bennett, all clean-cut yumminess in faded jeans, a black T-shirt and aviator sunglasses, standing on her stoop.

God, he was pretty.

Then again, looks weren't everything.

A fact she understood better than most.

"Hello, Quinn," he said, using her name as if he knew damn well hearing him say it made her insides go all soft and squishy.

As if he knew, exactly, what she'd done after he'd left her a quivering mass of unfulfilled desire last night. How she'd thought of him as she'd lain in bed. How she'd wished he was with her.

She leaned against the doorjamb—not exactly blocking the entrance, but not opening her arms wide and inviting him in, either. "Do you and your brother do everything together?"

He grinned, slow and sexy, and that soft, squishiness in her belly warmed. "Not everything, no."

The way he said it made it clear there was one very important thing they didn't do together.

Which was fine by her. She'd never been big on the whole ménage à trois thing. She preferred sex to be one-on-one.

Xander cleared his throat. Shifted. "There a reason you're asking about Zane?"

His tone was casual. Too casual. It bothered him, she realized, her bringing up his brother.

Men. Such sensitive creatures.

"I didn't ask about Zane," she pointed out. "I was just… curious about the whole wonder-twin power thing."

Mainly because ninety minutes ago, twin number one had stood in the exact same spot that twin number two currently occupied.

"Curious," Xander repeated flatly, his expression set. "About Zane. The same way you were curious last night?"

She remembered what she'd said to Xander last night when she'd pressed for his kiss.

I want to appease my curiosity.

"No," she said, for some reason not wanting Xander to think she had the same level of interest in Zane that she held for him. "Not the same. Not at all."

But she didn't tell him Zane had been here. That he'd flirted with her last night at the bar. That she'd flirted back.

A girl was entitled to a few secrets, after all.

"Now it's your turn," she continued when he remained silent. "You get to answer one of my questions. Like…oh, I don't know, why are you here?"

"I brought you something."

He thrust a small plastic bag at her. Her gaze narrowed. He and Zane had to be psychically linked.

Because Zane had brought her something, too. A cupcake from the Little Creek Bakery, a gorgeous cupcake topped with whipped cream, a perfectly ripe strawberry and glittery sprinkles. It had almost been too pretty to eat.

She had eaten it, of course. She wasn't an idiot.

It had tasted even better than it looked.

She took the bag and reached inside. Stared at the object. Zane had brought her a pretty, sweet treat and Xander had brought her…

"A dead bolt?" She looked from the dead bolt to him and back again. "You're giving me a dead bolt. Wow. And it's not even my birthday."

"It's for your door."

"Yes. I figured that. I didn't think you wanted me to put it on my shorts."

He blushed, either due to his stating the obvious or her smartass reply. Color climbed his neck. Stained his cheeks.

It was adorable.

"You need one," he said then cursed under his breath.

"On the door. One well-placed kick and anyone could get through the regular lock."

"I'll take your word for it as I don't have all that much door-kicking experience." She handed him the dead bolt. "Have at it. But I hope you brought your own toolbox. I don't have one. The last time I had to tighten a screw, I used a butter knife."

"I did. But I'm not installing it." He gave it back to her. "You are."

"Yet another thing I don't have any experience with." And not what she had planned on her list of things to do today. "Sorry."

"I'll teach you. And we'll go over a few self-defense moves. Carrying pepper spray is great—and smart," he added quickly, "but you need to be able to protect yourself in case an attacker gets physical."

Tucking a loose strand of hair behind her ear, she studied him. "You want to show me how to install a dead bolt and give me a lesson in self-defense?" He nodded. "Don't you have better things to do? Like spend time with your family or see your old friends or, I don't know, drive around town, soaking up the memories?"

He took off his sunglasses and met her eyes. "There's nothing I'd rather be doing, nowhere I'd rather be."

It was a line. It had to be. But it was a good one and, God, the way he said it like that with warmth in his eyes, sincerity in his tone...

She couldn't help but believe him.

Couldn't help but trust him.

Despite the little voice inside her head screaming at her not to.

SHE WAS A fast learner, Xander thought later.

Fast enough that he barely evaded having his balls shoved up to his throat by her knee.

"Good," he told her, rolling out of the way when she went for his eyes.

She had the right take-no-prisoners attitude and decent muscle tone in her long, lean body. But they'd been at it since she'd finished installing the dead bolt almost forty-five minutes ago and she was getting tired.

And that led to being sloppy. To making mistakes.

"That's enough for today," he said, and she collapsed into a heap on her living room floor.

"Oh, thank God." Her breathing was heavy and did some really interesting things to her tight tank top. "I thought the only way to get you to stop was by killing you, and I didn't want to get any bloodstains in here. I'm hoping to get my deposit back on this place."

He went into the kitchen and found the glasses in an upper cabinet. After filling one with water from the faucet, he went back to the living room, crouched down and handed it to her.

With a groan she sat up and took the glass. Sipped. "Thanks."

"You don't plan on staying here?"

"Here as in this apartment? Or here as in Little Creek?" She shook her head. "Never mind. Doesn't matter, as the answer to both is no. I'm only back in town temporarily."

"Until…?"

Her mouth flattened and he didn't think she'd answer. That she'd evade or change the subject like she did whenever he asked her a personal question. Whenever he got too close.

Instead, she surprised him.

"Until I pay off my debts." She gave a stiff, uncomfortable shrug. "Contrary to popular belief, getting a divorce isn't always the cheap and easy option. At least it wasn't either in my case. But it was still worth it. Even if I never manage to climb out this financial hole I dug for myself."

Taking her free hand, he tugged her to her feet, the move bringing their bodies flush. Desire flashed through him, hard and fast. He tamped it down. "You will."

"Oh? You're a fortune-teller now?"

"I don't have to see the future," he said, unable to hide the huskiness of his tone. He slid his hand up her arm then down again, reveling in her small tremble. "I see you. And you can do anything you set your mind to."

Her soft exhale was shaky. "You make it so hard," she murmured.

Biting his cheek so he didn't smile, he nodded. "Ditto."

She stilled for a moment then burst out laughing. He grinned. He liked making her laugh.

He liked it a lot.

"I meant you make it hard for me to remember to be smart. When you say things like that, when you look at me that way…you make me feel like the girl I used to be." She shook her head and stepped back, out of his arms. "But I can't be her anymore. I don't want to be her."

"You're the same person, Quinn. People don't change. Not completely."

It was the wrong thing to say. Her mouth thinned and she crossed her arms. "I have. I won't go back. Not for anything."

Not for you.

She didn't say it but he heard her meaning loud and clear.

"Was she so bad?" he asked softly. "The girl you used to be?"

Something flashed in her eyes, something that told him she missed that girl more than she was willing to admit. "She wasn't real. That's what you don't get. What no one got. She was whatever people wanted her to be, whoever they needed her to be. I'm just me. No longer gullible or willing to play a part. No longer reckless."

He pulled her to him once more, the move slow enough, easy enough that she could stop it any time she wanted.

She didn't.

He settled his hands on her waist, slid his fingers under the hem of her tank top and lightly caressed her warm, soft skin. "What's life without a little risk?"

"Safe," she whispered. "It's safe."

"Sounds boring."

She rolled her eyes and once again slipped away from him, this time to carry her glass into the kitchen. "Says the man who gets shot at for a living."

He followed her, leaning against the partition separating the rooms as she put her glass in the sink. "Not every day."

Though on more occasions than he could admit.

Mainly because most of those times had been classified missions.

"Yeah, well, boring or not, I'm going to stick with it." She sent him a long look over her shoulder. "But that's not to say I'm against finding myself a little excitement when the mood strikes."

"A *little* excitement?"

"Well, I'm hoping it's at least average-sized, but a girl never can tell."

"Hoping?" he asked, not about to set her straight on the size of his excitement. It would sound like bragging. Or lying. "Does that mean the mood has struck?"

"Now who's the one who's hoping?"

"It's what gets me through the day."

She laughed. "How about we just say that I'm…considering my options."

Considering her options. At least she wasn't kicking his ass to the curb.

He'd take it.

And do everything in his power to make sure that after she'd considered those options, she chose him.

6

SHE OWED HIM. that was what Quinn told herself an hour later as she walked down Main Street with Xander, the sun shining brightly overhead. She owed him for bringing her that dead bolt and for the self-defense lesson. That was the only reason she'd agreed to go with him, to help him shop for a present for his sister.

Okay, okay. So maybe it wasn't the *only* reason. She liked being with him. He was quiet, yes, but when he spoke—dear Lord, when he spoke—the things he said? They resonated.

His words burrowed inside of her, warm and bright, like she'd swallowed the sun.

I see you. And you can do anything you set your mind to.

How was a girl supposed to resist that?

Why would she want to?

But that didn't mean she was going to toss aside her caution. Considering her options, that was all she was doing.

She glanced at him. And if she enjoyed the view—and his company—while she did so? Well, that was just an added bonus.

"What about something from the bakery?" she asked as they came upon the building with its new striped awning. She had firsthand experience of how good their cup-cakes were.

Not that she planned on mentioning Zane again. She didn't have any brothers or sisters so she didn't understand the whole sibling-rivalry thing, but when she'd brought up Zane's name—innocently—Xander's expression had said it all.

He didn't want her talking about his brother. It was almost as if he was...jealous.

Which she didn't want, she assured herself even as pure feminine delight went through her. She was too old for high school games, pitting one guy against another. And she didn't want Zane.

She should, she thought with a frown. He was exactly the type of guy she usually went for. The type of guy she used to go for. Charming and fun and that sexy bad-boy edge didn't hurt, either.

But maybe... She slid another glance at Xander, the sun shining on his light hair, his eyes once again hidden behind sunglasses. Maybe there was something to be said for the boy-next-door thing.

Who knew?

Xander stopped and considered the bakery, then shook his head.

Quinn raised her eyebrows. "Chocolate?" she asked. "There's a candy store down the block."

"No."

"Okay. What about flowers?"

He snorted. "So she can shove them up my ass?" he muttered. "No, thanks."

"Hold on, hold on," Quinn said, touching his arm to get him to stop, a thought occurring to her. "What did you do?"

"What?"

"To your sister," she clarified, suspicion lacing her tone.

Which made sense as she was becoming mighty suspicious. "You said she was angry with you, but you didn't say why."

Quinn didn't know Kerri Bennett—now Kerri Finch—all that well, but from what she remembered, Kerri was a perfectly nice woman. And not the type to shove flowers up anybody's ass.

Taking off his sunglasses, Xander stepped closer, his brow lowered, his voice soft. And angry. "I don't lie."

The vehemence in his tone, the way he read her so damn easily, had her back going up. "I didn't say you did."

"You didn't have to. You think I made up the story about needing help picking out a gift for my sister so I could spend more time with you, but that's not how I work. I don't lie," he repeated. "I don't cheat. And when I want to spend time with a woman, I tell her. No games. No excuses."

And now she felt like the idiot she'd insisted just last night she wasn't. "So you don't want to spend time with me?"

"You have no idea what I want."

Oh, my. She swallowed and licked her lips, her next words out before she could think them through. "Tell me."

Something hot and wicked flashed in his eyes. "I want to get to know you. Your fears and dreams and goals. What you like. What you don't. What you think and feel." He stepped closer, his voice dropping to a low, husky growl that scraped across her nerve endings. "I want to kiss you again. I want to touch you. Taste you. I want to make you come with my fingers. With my tongue. And then, when you're weak with pleasure, your body quivering with it, I want to do it all over again."

God. God! He didn't have to wait—she felt plenty weak now, arousal snaking through her system, dampening her panties. She could picture him doing all of the above with a skill she was certain would leave her not only quivering but begging for more.

He'd leave and she'd be left wanting more.

She'd be left alone.

"I'm not your ex," he said, as if reading her mind, "or any of the other guys who hurt you, Quinn."

She dropped her gaze, her heart racing. "I'm trying," she blurted, forcing herself to meet his eyes. "I'm trying to trust you. Doesn't that count for something?"

He sighed. "It counts." Taking her lightly by the elbow, he steered her down the sidewalk. Nodded curtly at a woman a few years younger than them who greeted him with a hopeful "I'd like to eat you up" smile. "This morning, I may have asked Kerri if she thought eating three slices of French toast swimming in butter and syrup was the best decision."

Once again Quinn stopped. This time in shock. "You told a pregnant woman she was fat? Holy cow," she breathed. "You're either the bravest man alive. Or the dumbest."

He squeezed the back of his neck, shifted his weight. "I didn't say she was fat. The word *fat* never came out of my mouth."

"It may as well have."

"What was I supposed to do? When I called her a month ago she started blubbering about some hurtful comment her doctor made about her weight during her checkup. I was just trying to save her from herself."

"She didn't want you to save her. She just wanted you to listen, maybe offer up a few words of encouragement and/or commiseration."

His shoulders hunched. "Now you tell me."

He looked so miserable, so embarrassed and remorseful, Quinn about melted into a puddle of lust and longing and growing affection at his feet.

Not good. Not good at all.

But she couldn't seem to stop it from happening. Just as she couldn't stop herself from what she did next.

"Come on," she said, taking him by the hand and tugging him to the curb. She checked for traffic then stepped onto the crosswalk. "I know the perfect gift."

QUINN'S PERFECT GIFT came at a price.

But dropping a couple hundred bucks was a small price to pay if it meant earning Kerri's forgiveness.

Plus, it had the added benefit of Quinn helping him.

No, he wouldn't make up an excuse to get her to spend more time with him.

But that didn't mean he'd turn one down if he happened to have a good one.

They walked out of the spa side by side, which wasn't as good as walking in hand in hand, but Quinn was still with him, had initiated that hand holding, was talking and smiling up at him.

He'd take it. He'd take all of it.

But what he wanted to take most of all was her.

"You think an afternoon in there is long enough?" he asked as they headed back toward his truck, walking close enough that their arms brushed. "She might need a day or two." He glanced at Quinn. "She holds a grudge."

"Are you afraid of her?"

"Terrified," he told her honestly. "She has a mean streak."

"I thought she was a kindergarten teacher?"

He nodded solemnly. "She hides it well."

As he'd hoped, Quinn laughed. "After a few hours of being pampered, she'll be a new woman." She nudged him with her hip. "Better yet, she'll forget all about wanting to kill you."

"Maybe. But I'm still sleeping with one eye open while I'm here."

"It must be nice, seeing your family. Spending time with them."

"It's great." It didn't happen nearly enough, but it was the life both he and Zane had chosen. Luckily, their mom and Kerri had always supported their decisions. He remembered what Quinn had told him about missing her mom. "You said you weren't planning on staying in Little Creek. Will you move to Seattle when you leave?"

"I'm not sure. It doesn't matter where I go, really. I just need someplace where I can figure out what to do next. Who to be."

"Is that why you're taking online courses? So you can figure out who you want to be?" When she frowned at him, he shrugged. "I noticed the textbooks on your table."

"Nothing gets past you, does it?"

She didn't sound happy about it—or about him knowing she was taking online college courses—and he wondered if she was angry. Or embarrassed.

"I think it's great that you're working on your degree."

"It's no big deal," she said, her cheeks pink. "It's just a few business courses."

Taking hold of her arm, he stopped her. Turned her to face him. "It's great. You should be proud of yourself for going after what you want."

"I'm not sure it is what I want. But it's the best way for me to prove Peter wrong."

Peter. Her ex. The idiot who'd cheated on her.

"Prove him wrong how?" he asked, having a feeling that he wasn't going to like what she was about to say.

She tugged free of his hold and crossed her arms.

"When we were first married, I told him I wanted to take some classes at the community college but he refused to pay for it. Said my brain wasn't my strongest asset and me trying to get an education would be a waste of time and his money."

Xander's hands fisted. Nope. He didn't like it. Not one bit. "He was wrong."

And an asshole, but he was sure she was aware of that.

Still, she looked so wounded, he took her by the shoulders and leaned in, holding her gaze. "He. Was. Wrong."

"I stayed with him," she blurted, gripping his forearms. "He thought so little of me, he lied and he cheated, and I still stayed with him."

In that moment, Xander would have given anything for ol' Petey's address. The bastard deserved a good beating for hurting Quinn. For making her doubt herself.

"But you did leave. You're here and you're living life on your own terms." He softened his tone, his thumbs caressing her upper arms. "You're smart and you're strong. Stronger than him. Stronger than your mistakes. Now you just need to be strong enough to forgive yourself for those mistakes."

FORGIVE HERSELF? Quinn wasn't sure she knew how.

Was afraid she wasn't capable.

Because forgiveness might lead to forgetting. She could get complacent. Could slip back into old habits. Could go back to being the woman she'd been—married for her looks, expected to sit still, look pretty and be quiet. Back to the princess who'd craved attention and adoration.

But gazing into Xander's eyes, listening to him, it was easy, so very easy, to forget all that. To believe in the possibilities.

The possibility of getting her college degree.

The possibility of paying back every last cent she owed. The possibility of moving on. Of trusting a man again. Of falling in love.

She jerked, her breath catching.

So much for being smart. For being careful.

"Quinn?" Xander murmured, watching her with a frown.

She stepped back, forcing him to let go. "I have to go home," she said, proud of her cool tone. "My shift starts soon and I need to get ready."

More like she needed some space, some time alone to shore up her resolve, to remember what was important.

They were silent on the ride back to her place—her doing, she knew, as she stared out the passenger-side window, kept her thoughts to herself.

Where they belonged.

He'd barely pulled to a stop in front of her apartment when she unbuckled her seat belt and reached for the door handle.

"I'll wait," he said before she could get out. "We'll go register for the reunion together, then I'll drop you off at Myer's."

"I'm not going to the reunion." Yes, yes, she was supposed to go, had agreed in a weak moment to hand out the award for most valuable graduates to Zane and Xander. But she couldn't go through with it. The lines between past and present were blurring too much already. Attending the reunion would only make things worse. "So no need to register," she continued. "And no need for you to wait. I'll walk to work, like I always do."

No sense changing that now. She might get some stupid, crazy idea. Like that just because she could count on him once for something as simple and silly as a ride to work, she could count on him for other things, too.

"You're skipping the reunion?" he asked with a frown. "Why?"

"I have to work." Which wasn't technically true. At least, not yet, but she'd make sure it happened. As soon as she got to the bar, she'd ask Dianne to add her to the schedule for that night. "And I have no desire to relive my high school days." She opened the door. "Thanks for—"

"Have dinner with me."

She froze. "Working. Remember?"

"Tomorrow then." He paused and the air in the cab thickened. Heated. He touched her, his fingers brushing against the nape of her neck, and she shut her eyes against a fierce wave of longing. "I want to see you again, Quinn."

She wanted that, too. Wanted it so much.

And that was the problem.

She faced him. His hand curved around the back of her neck and she knew, if she didn't tell him the truth, he'd pull her to him. That he'd kiss her and she'd be powerless to resist.

"I already have plans tomorrow," she told him. "With Zane."

His fingers tensed and he quickly yanked his hand away. Fisted it around the steering wheel as he stared out the windshield, his expression hard. "When?"

"Tomor—"

"No," he ground out. "When did he ask you out?" He looked at her, his eyes narrowed. "Or did you ask him?"

"I… He asked me." Had invited her to coffee, an innocent coffee date in the middle of the day. But Xander didn't need to know that. Her palms were damp and she wiped them down the front of her shorts. "He came over this afternoon. Before you did."

"He came over," Xander repeated flatly, "today, and

asked you out and you said yes. After I kissed you last night. After you kissed me."

It wasn't a question, but she answered it anyway. "Yes."

He turned away from her again.

Just like she knew he would.

Wasn't that why she was telling him this? She was testing him. She needed him to back off. She was falling for him—too hard. Too fast. She needed some space so she'd done what she'd had to do.

But she hadn't meant to hurt him.

"Xander, I…" She stopped. She had no idea what to say. What to do. Once again, she'd gotten herself into a mess she had no idea how to get out of.

"You'd better go," he said, still not looking at her. "You don't want to be late for work."

It was a dismissal. One delivered in a cold, angry tone he hadn't used with her before.

One she knew damn well she deserved.

"Goodbye, Xander," she said around the lump in her throat.

She climbed out, shut the door and walked up to her apartment, feeling him watch her as she went. It wasn't until she was safely inside, the door shut, blocking her from his view, that she let her head hang. Her shoulders droop.

She'd wanted to push him away.

Mission accomplished.

7

When Quinn stepped out of Myer's the next night, she spied Xander leaning against his truck under a streetlight.

Everything within her stilled only to start up again in a rush of pure adrenaline.

And no little amount of desire.

For a moment, she wondered if she was hallucinating, if she'd somehow conjured him up with her imagination. After all, ever since he'd driven away from her apartment yesterday, she'd thought of him. Had looked for him both that evening at work and tonight, her heart in her throat every time the door opened, hoping he'd walk in, that he'd sit at the bar and watch her. That he'd offer to take her home.

He hadn't.

So she wasn't quite sure whether or not to believe what she was seeing.

Until he spoke. "You're done early."

Yes, that was definitely his deep voice. He was real. He was here.

She wasn't sure whether to turn and run like hell.

Or throw herself into his arms.

She did neither, just crossed the empty street. "Steve's closing tonight. What are you doing here?"

He straightened, his voice soft and husky and honest in the night. "You know what I'm doing here."

Her knees went weak. Yes, yes, she knew damn well what he was doing. What he wanted.

She wanted it, too.

She'd dreamed of him this morning, a hot, wicked dream of them together in her bed. Of his hands on her breasts. Between her legs. Had fantasized about him while she was in the shower, the water pulsing against her sensitized skin.

The man was altogether too tempting. Dangerous to her self-control.

But she no longer cared. She wanted him. More than she wanted to protect herself.

Mostly, though, she'd missed him.

It didn't make sense, but there you had it. They'd spent such little time together, but she missed hearing him talk, the way he looked at her, how he listened.

She liked being with him. She just liked him, period.

And she was so very tired of being alone.

Tonight, it seemed, she didn't have to be.

"Take me home."

By THE TIME he followed her into her apartment, Quinn's stomach was a jumble of nerves. Xander hadn't spoken. When she told him to take her home, he'd simply held the passenger-side door open. He'd stayed silent during the drive, climbing out after he'd parked in front of her apartment and circling the truck to open her door, then following her inside. Now he stood inside her apartment by the door, as if he was unsure of his welcome.

As if he was unsure whether or not he wanted to stay.

"Do you want a drink?" she asked, hating that she was so nervous her voice shook.

This wasn't the first time she'd brought a man home, for God's sake. She was close to thirty, had dated plenty before meeting Peter, had been married and divorced. She wasn't some trembling, hesitant virgin. She was a strong, confident, sensual woman who just happened to have been on a self-imposed sexual sabbatical for the past year.

Still, there was no need for her heart to be racing. Her stomach jittery.

He hadn't even touched her yet.

"Or," she continued, deciding the best way to calm her anxiety was to take matters into her own hands, which she did by sliding her hands up his chest then linking her fingers behind his neck, "we could skip the drink."

But when she rose onto her toes to press her mouth to his, he leaned back. "My brother…"

Letting go of him, she fell back to her heels. "I thought you said you and your brother didn't do everything together."

His mouth thinned at her lame attempt at humor. "You were with him today. You went out with him."

Damn it. This was her own fault for telling him about Zane inviting her out.

Her own fault for going.

"It was only coffee," she said. "We spent an hour at the local café. We caught up, chatted a bit. It was nothing."

"Nothing," Xander repeated flatly. Obviously it was something to him.

She needed to remember that.

"Are you going to see him again?" he asked.

"No." But he didn't seem convinced so she repeated it. "No. I…" She shook her head, irritated and scared and knowing she had to make this right. "I don't want Zane," she whispered, telling him the truth. She didn't want his brother. And if their coffee date had been any indication, he wasn't interested in her, either. Oh, they'd had a nice enough time, but that was all it was. Nice. Two old classmates catching up with each other. There'd been no sparks. No connection.

Nothing even remotely close to what she felt when she was with Xander.

Taking a chance, she touched him again, laying her hand on his chest, settling it there, over his heart. "I want you."

And admitting that was among the hardest things she'd ever done. Standing there, waiting for him to accept—or reject—her?

Torture.

Which she was sure he damn well knew.

"I want you," she repeated. "You've gotten under my skin. In my head. The whole time I was with Zane, I thought of you. I can't stop thinking about you." She frowned at him. "It's annoying as hell."

"That what this is? A way for you to try to get me out of your system?"

"Yes. No." She shook her head. "That's part of it."

"Part? What's the rest?"

She took a deep breath. "The rest is that I've finished considering my options, and while I'm still not sure this is a smart idea, I'm willing to take the risk. I want to take it. With you."

SHE WANTED HIM.

Quinn's words, the reality of what she'd said hit Xander hard, like a punch to the gut.

But he couldn't take what she was offering. Couldn't give what she wanted. Something was holding him back.

Mainly the jealousy eating away at him.

Goddamn his idiot friends, this stupid challenge and his

brother's competitive streak. Zane had never shown any interest in Quinn before and Xander suspected he had no real interest in her now, wouldn't have invited her out for coffee if not for the challenge.

Then again, if it hadn't been for the challenge, if he hadn't known that Zane would take it seriously and try to get Quinn to go to the reunion with him, Xander might not have gone after her himself.

Maybe he should be grateful for his idiot friends and the stupid challenge.

And he would be, he promised himself. Later. Much, much later.

"I couldn't stay away," he admitted, wondering how she'd gotten him so tangled up in such a short time. "I tried. I really did..."

"You stayed away last night," she pointed out, and beyond the irritation in her eyes, he saw the hurt.

"It wasn't easy." But he'd been pissed. Had managed to keep it together, to keep it under wraps during the reunion registration while Zane had bragged about bringing Quinn a freaking cupcake and they'd learned about the parade in their honor. He held her gaze. "But it was what you wanted."

She opened her mouth. Shut it. "More like I wanted to see if you'd stay away."

Her confession rocked him. He almost had. He'd known her telling him about Zane was her way of putting distance between them.

She'd pushed him away.

He'd let her. Had almost convinced himself that walking away was for the best. For both of them.

But he didn't give up. Not when he wanted something. Not when it mattered.

"You're under my skin, too," he told her gruffly, setting his hands on her hips and drawing her closer. "In my head."

She shut her eyes briefly as if in relief, then laid her other hand on his chest, too. Tilted her face up to his. "Trying to get me out of your system?" she asked, a teasing glint in her eyes.

"Going to try." He skimmed one hand up her side, his fingertips trailing over her tank top—red tonight—grazing the bumps of her rib cage, then the soft swell of her breast and over her clavicle bone. Sliding his hand up the silky skin of her throat, he curled it around the back of her neck and fisted her hair in his hand. Tugged her head back. "But it'll probably take a few times."

She once again linked her hands behind his neck. "Probably?"

"Definitely," he murmured, lowering his head. He brushed his mouth against hers. "It will most definitely take a few times."

He kissed her, the taste of her roaring through him, the feel of her—hips and stomach and breasts—against him like fuel on a fire. Having his arms around her, kissing her, had desire heating his veins, his body hardening.

The hold he had on his control slipped but he shored it up. He wanted to take his time. Hell, it wasn't every day a man had the chance to take his fantasy woman to bed. He wasn't going to rush it.

He kissed her, again and again and again, slow and deep, his tongue sliding against hers languidly. He slipped the hand at her hip under the hem of her shirt, caressed the slope of her waist. She was warm and soft and clung to him, her core pressed against his growing arousal. She rolled her hips and he groaned, set both hands on her waist to keep her still.

To keep himself in check. In control.

"Mmm," she murmured against his mouth before breaking the kiss and leaning back. "It's not going to work, you know."

"It'll work," he promised. "Trust me."

She laughed and if possible, he got even harder. "I'm sure it will but that's not what I'm talking about. I'm talking about you trying to slow us down." She nipped at his chin then soothed the sting with a soft, wet kiss. "I don't want to go slow. I don't want you careful and sweet. Not the first time. It's been such a long time for me and I have such a hunger for you," she murmured, and had the blood roaring in his ears.

Stepping back, she cupped her breasts, rubbed her thumbs over the tips with a soft moan. "I need your mouth here." She brushed her fingers over her core, sliding one fingertip up then down before cupping him through his jeans. "I want you inside of me. Hard, fast and deep." She rubbed him and he swelled under her hand. "Now. Right now."

And like that, the tenuous thread of his control snapped. He yanked her to him, bringing her to her toes, whirled them around so that her back was pressed against the wall and prepared to give his woman everything she asked for.

Yes, QUINN THOUGHT WILDLY, this…this was what she wanted. What she craved. Xander kissing her, his mouth hungry and rough, his hands on her, his body pressing against hers. But it wasn't enough. Wasn't nearly enough.

She matched the ferocity of his kiss, worked her hands between them to cup him once again. He pushed himself more fully into her hand and she fumbled with the tab on his jeans, tugged down the zipper.

He stepped back, and for a moment she was afraid he was going to stop her, try to slow them down again, but instead he reached over his head and yanked his shirt off and tossed it aside. Oh, dear Lord, the man was gorgeous, all sharply cut muscles and smooth, golden skin, but before she could look her fill, he was kissing her again, his hands molding her breasts.

Since she didn't have the luxury of soaking him in, she took the opportunity to touch him, sliding her hands up his ridged abs to the hard planes of his chest and down again before dipping her hand beneath the waistband of his briefs.

Breaking the kiss, breathing hard, he pressed his forehead against hers as she circled him. He was smooth and hot and hard—and way, way bigger than average. She ran the pad of her thumb over his tip, drawing the bead of moisture around the head, then stroked him. He groaned.

He trembled.

A heady rush of feminine power raced through her that she could make this incredible man tremble with wanting her. That she could make such a strong man weak just by touching him.

That she could make him lose control.

Shoving him back a step, she pulled off her tank top then kicked off her shoes and shimmied out of her jeans, standing before him in only her red silky bra and a matching thong.

"So hungry for you," she murmured, repeating her words from a moment ago.

She pushed his jeans and underwear down slowly, then knelt before him. His cock jutted out, thick and heavy, the head glistening.

"Quinn."

Her name on his lips was a question. A plea.

She smiled up at him.

Then took him in her mouth.

With a moan, he tipped his head back, his hands fisted at his sides. She gripped the backs of his thighs, the muscles like steel, the skin covering them warm, and took him in deeper. His hands shot to her head, his fingers tangling in her hair, his grip on her light. Reverent.

Though she was on her knees, she didn't feel submissive. She felt strong. She reveled in it, in him sharing in this strength, giving her this moment of control. He moved just a little, pushing farther into her mouth then withdrawing. He did it again. Then again.

She looked up at him, saw what it was taking for him to hold back, the cost of that control, his jaw tight, his eyes narrowed as he watched her. And she wanted, more than anything, to give him what he craved. What he needed. She worked him, breathing in his musky scent, the salty taste of him on her tongue. Again and again, she slid her lips over him until he gave a low, vicious curse and pulled her to her feet.

He kissed her like a madman, like a man possessed, and she matched him, licking her way into his mouth, scraping her teeth against his lower lip. His erection pressed against her belly and she wiggled, trying to ease the ache between her thighs. Reaching down for his jeans, he pulled a condom from his pocket and sheathed himself, then slid a hand under the string of her thong and in one swift move, yanked it back, ripping it in two.

Excitement coursed through her. He lifted her and she wrapped her legs around his waist. Pressing her back against the wall, still kissing her, he guided himself inside her. She bucked her hips, needing more.

"Xander," she gasped, clutching his shoulders. "Please."

Shifting her to one arm, he reached between them and stroked her clit. "That's it," he said, his words a low growl. "Come for me. Come for me."

She did, her entire body shaking, her head tipped back. Wave after wave of pleasure coursed through her, left her breathless.

Boneless, her legs started to slide off him but he hefted her higher, the move seating him even deeper. "No," he said roughly. "We're not done. Not by a long shot."

Taking her butt in his hands, he plunged into her again and again, hard and fast and deep, giving her everything she wanted. Pressure built, coiled inside of her like a spring and she crossed her ankles, dug her heels into his lower back trying to find purchase. Searching for release.

He kissed her neck, her collarbone. The slope of her breasts. "Again." He widened his stance and moved faster. Harder. "Again."

She was helpless. Helpless against his husky command, against the feel of him, so thick and hot moving inside her.

But she wasn't in this alone.

"Not alone," she said, sliding her hands into his hair and nudging his head up. She met his eyes. "I want you there with me. Right with me."

Pulling him down for her kiss, she stroked her tongue into his mouth and gave him all she had. All she was. Her hips moved like a piston, meeting him thrust for thrust. Her legs tightened around him like a vise, holding him as close as her own skin. His grip on her changed and he drew her higher, tipping her slightly so that her back arched, her hair caught between her shoulder blades and the wall. But she didn't mind the sharp tug, could only think of one thing.

"Please," she breathed, close, so very close to the edge of pleasure of again. "Please, please, please, please…"

Unbelievably, incredibly, she felt him grow even harder, and her orgasm swept over her like a wave. She cried out, her body quaking. As she crested the top of it, he followed, giving her everything he was with a short, guttural moan.

And when he held her after, his face pressed against the crook of her neck, their breathing heavy, their bodies slick with sweat, she smoothed her hands across his shoulders.

No, she wasn't alone.

Not tonight.

8

XANDER'S FEET POUNDED against the sidewalk, his breathing deep and even, though he was on mile five of his run. Routine was important. Doing the same thing, repeating a task over and over, staying on top of one's game kept a man sharp, kept a warrior's instincts honed. So today he got up at 0500 for PT like he did every morning.

Like he did most every morning, he amended. He'd spent the past three mornings—and nights and two afternoons—in Quinn's bed.

But now he was back on track, doing what he needed to do.

Too bad doing what he needed to do meant he'd left a gorgeous, naked woman alone in her bed last night.

He gritted his teeth. Yeah, he was a goddamn idiot.

This was for her, too, he told himself as he headed toward the high school. She was at Myer's till after midnight, and he kept her up even later, trying to appease his hunger for her. It wasn't working, and he was afraid it never would—something he'd worry about later.

No, he'd done the right thing, sneaking out of her bed after she'd fallen asleep, leaving a lame note on the table telling her he'd call her later. He was monopolizing her time. She had a life here in Little Creek that she needed to get back to. Work and her studies and friends…

He frowned and wiped the sweat from his forehead. Not that she'd ever mentioned any friends, but she had to have some. She was smart and fun with a wicked sense of humor. But she never talked about anyone. Never had any calls or texts, never made plans to meet up for lunch.

What the hell was up with that?

In high school, she'd been constantly surrounded by people. Was always the center of attention, the sun in a circling group of kids vying for some of her warmth. Her brightness.

Now she was alone.

He picked up his pace. Her choice, he told himself. She was the one who kept herself so guarded. But she'd let him in. Was letting him get close.

And it was messing with his head.

Another reason he'd needed to go on this run. He needed to sort through the twisting, turning thoughts in his mind.

Like why he'd had such a hard time leaving her bed a few hours ago. Why he'd spent a good thirty minutes watching her after she'd fallen asleep last night.

Why he'd spent those thirty minutes mentally going over how much leave he had left this year, how often he could come back to Little Creek to see her again.

Yeah, he needed to figure a few things out. And he would. That was what he did. Zane was the impulsive one. He went with his gut, followed his instincts. Xander thought things through. Went over his options. Considered each and every possible outcome.

And falling for Quinn Oswald hadn't made the list.

Xander stopped—just put on the brakes, his momentum almost carrying him forward into a somersault. His heart raced, his breath heaved out and he knew damn well it had nothing to do with his run, but with that crazy, wayward notion.

He hadn't fallen for her. Yes, she was beautiful and sexy, and the sex was everything he'd fantasized about and more. He frowned, began a slow jog around the front of the school. But she was more than his fantasy. Better than some hot, sweaty dream. Some magical ideal he'd worked up of her in his head.

She was real.

And he wanted her in his life—not just for the rest of his leave but for weeks…months…maybe even years to come.

He picked up his pace as if he could outrun the truth. He *had* fallen for her.

Now he was stuck trying to figure out how to handle that information.

And what to do next.

HE'D LEFT HER a note.

A neatly printed, properly structured, grammatically correct note written on the back of an envelope.

Quinn almost kept it.

That was how far gone she was, she thought, forcing herself to rip the envelope in half then stacking the two pieces together and ripping it again. So far gone that for a moment, she'd seriously contemplated keeping a piece of junk mail just because Xander had written on it. It wasn't a love note, for God's sake. It was an "I'm leaving" note.

And she needed to take it for what it was. Had to take his sneaking out of her bed while she slept for what that was, too.

Goodbye.

Oh, sure, the note had said that he'd call her later, but she wasn't an idiot.

Or maybe she was, she thought, pouring herself a cup

of coffee and taking a sip. Because she'd been surprised to find the note. Had been disappointed when she'd woken in her bed alone.

She'd reached for him. Her eyes hadn't even been open and she'd reached for him.

She'd counted on him being there.

That must be what they meant by a rude awakening.

But she was awake now, her eyes wide-open to what was happening.

What she and Xander had was winding down.

She curled up on her sofa and stared blankly out the small window overlooking the street. She'd known this would happen. The man was a SEAL. He had a career. Missions to accomplish, freedom to protect, the whole bit. He sure couldn't do that from Little Creek. They were temporary. There was no other way they could be. He lived in Virginia. She lived here. He had a career and plans for his future while she was floundering, trying to figure out what to do with her life. Who to be.

They weren't meant to last more than a few weeks. She'd known this day, this moment of them being over would come.

She just hadn't realized it would hurt this much.

Lesson learned.

One she needed to keep firmly in mind, she resolved as Xander pulled up and parked then jumped out of his truck, a man on a mission in running shorts and a T-shirt, his stride long and purposeful, his expression set.

Well, she was on a mission, too.

Protect her heart at all cost.

Determined to do just that, she got to her feet and hurried over and opened the door—despite wearing only a tank top and black-cotton boy briefs. Her heart—the very same one she was so adamant about protecting—tumbled at the sight of him, his shirt clinging to his chest, his hair damp with sweat.

She glanced up at the heavens. She could use a little help here.

"Did you forget something?" she asked, so proud of her cool, "couldn't care less if he ever came back or not" tone.

"Yes."

She raised her eyebrows at that one word, ground out from between his teeth. Why on earth was he mad? He'd left her.

She stepped aside but he didn't move. "Well? Come in and get it. And hurry. I was just about to take a shower." She gave him a slow once-over. Wrinkled her nose. "You might want to do the same."

He nodded once, stepped inside, shut the door.

And swept her up in his arms.

"What are you doing?" she asked as he carried her toward her bedroom.

She told herself the only reason she wasn't screeching at him was because she was breathless with shock—not excitement. That she didn't struggle because the man was a SEAL and any attempt she would make to extricate herself would only serve to bruise her dignity. And the only, only reason she linked her hands behind his neck and held on was so he didn't drop her.

If a woman couldn't lie to herself, who could she lie to?

Stepping into her room, he slid her an unreadable glance. "You told me to come in and take what I wanted." He shrugged as if he wasn't holding one hundred and fifteen pounds in his arms. "I'm taking what I want."

"I told you to come in and get what you forgot. It wasn't an invitation to pillage and plunder."

"I forgot you," he said, then he gave her a brief, hard

kiss that tasted of frustration and anger and something else she couldn't name, before tossing her on the bed.

She bounced and shoved the hair out of her face. Leaned her weight on her elbows and reclined on the bed, reveling in his hungry gaze. "You didn't *forget* me. You left me. Snuck out of here—" she patted the mattress "—like a thief in the night."

He toed off his sneakers, kicked them aside. "Didn't you get my note?"

"Oh, I got it."

"Then you knew I'd be back," he said, bending down to slide off his socks.

"How could I? Your note only said you'd call later."

"You knew I'd be back," he repeated, holding her gaze.

She hadn't. Not for certain. "I thought you'd had your fill," she blurted.

He straightened. Frowned. "What?"

Her face heated and she sat up. Crossed her arms over her chest. This was the problem with letting a man get too close. He made a woman weak. Made her clingy.

Made her want more and more of him.

"I thought maybe you'd worked me out of your system," she said, referencing the words from the other night before they'd made love for the first time.

He shook head. "Impossible. Under my skin, remember?" His voice softened, his gaze warmed. "In my head."

Giddiness flowed through her, followed by the most dangerous of all emotions.

Hope.

She tried to tamp it down but it kept rising, filling her chest with lightness. That sensation expanded when he spoke again.

"I can't stop thinking about you," he admitted, stripping off his shirt. "I can't stop wanting you." He stepped out of his shorts, standing before her with his arousal evident in a pair of clinging boxer briefs. Her mouth dried, her gaze glued to the movement as he slid them off, his cock jutting free. He stroked himself. "This is what you do to me. All I have to do is think about you and I'm hard and aching for you. Tell me you feel the same way," he said gruffly. "Tell me it's the same for you."

She shouldn't. Admitting that would give him even more power over her, and she was terrified he had too much as it was. But she couldn't deny him.

She couldn't deny him anything.

"It's the same," she whispered, her gaze glued to the movement of his hand, how he stroked himself lazily all while watching her. "Under my skin. In my head. All I have to do is think about you and I want you. Sometimes, the wanting gets to be too much, more than I can bear…" Times like now, her breasts tingling, her nipples hard. She squeezed her inner thighs together. "Like after you kissed me the first time."

He stilled, his entire body going rigid. "Quinn…"

"I thought of you," she told him, loving how his gaze darkened. His breathing ragged. "I thought of your hands, your mouth on me." She trailed her fingertips over the center of her panties where she was wet for him. "And I touched myself."

Letting go of his cock, hands fisted at his sides, he stepped closer. "Show me."

XANDER'S CHEST GREW tight as he waited to see if Quinn would comply with his demand. Eyes on his, she smiled, a slow, confident, purely feminine grin, then peeled her tank top off, tossing it aside. The movement made her breasts bounce.

His breath shuddered out.

"After you left that night," she said, her voice soft and husky, entrancing him with her words, with what she was about to do, "I couldn't sleep. I kept wondering if I should have asked you to stay. If I'd made the wrong decision in letting you go. And I…I ached." She pressed her palm to her center. "Here." Cupped her breasts. "Here. I tried to make it go away." She squeezed her breasts, plumping them up then running her thumbs around her areolas, her nipples jutting out.

His mouth watered with the need to taste them. To lick and suck them until she writhed beneath him. "But it wasn't enough."

She shook her head, kept her gaze on his. "It felt so good," she said, breathing heavier, her face flushed with desire. She pinched her nipples, rolled the peaks between her fingers with a groan that threatened to snap his control. "So…so good…"

Lying back, she slid one hand slowly down her stomach, her fingers trailing back and forth against the edge of her panties, then they dipped down, traced over her clit before moving back up. She repeated the movement. Then again. He was hypnotized, unable to move, unable to look away from that hand, those fingers teasing herself. Then she slipped her fingers under the waistband.

He moved like a shot, covering her hand with his. When her surprised gaze met his, he could barely speak but he forced the words out. "Let me see."

Nodding in understanding, she lifted her hips and he slid her panties off, giving in to his urge to touch her by trailing his fingertips down the backs of her legs. She combed her fingers through the short, curly hair there, at the apex of her thighs, and sighed. Pinched the nipple of her left breast and arched her back.

When her fingers delved deeper, parting her own folds,

he groaned and knew he'd never, ever forget the sight of her this way, her fingers playing with her breast, her hand between her thighs, her skin flushed with pleasure.

And when she came with a long, low moan he knew he couldn't hold on any longer.

She hadn't even come down from her orgasm when he crawled onto the bed, straddling her thighs. Bending his head, he kissed her, long and deep, then picked up her right hand.

And sucked her fingers into his mouth. He shut his eyes, the taste of her on his tongue only making him want more.

Much, much more.

He dipped his head and latched on to her breast, sucking until she gasped, his fingers working the other peak. Her hands trailed over his shoulders, delved into his hair and he grabbed them both, bracketed her wrists with one hand and held her arms over her head. He'd never last if she touched him.

She didn't have a headboard so he guided her hands to the edges of the mattress. Curled her fingers around it. "Don't let go."

Without waiting for her acquiescence, he slid back down, kissing her neck and the tips of both breasts, trailing his lips over her torso, swirling his tongue around her belly button. At the juncture of her thighs, he stopped. Inhaled her scent then blew lightly across her curls. Her stomach quivered.

"Open for me," he growled softly, glancing up at her, loving how she looked with her arms stretched overhead, breasts lifted. He blew on her again and she squirmed. "Let me in, Quinn."

She did, spreading her thighs, giving him a gift. One he planned on treasuring.

XANDER KISSED HER inner thighs. He hadn't shaved yet and his whiskers scraped lightly against her skin.

Quinn tightened her grip on the mattress, her body a mass of overly sensitized nerves. "Xander…please…"

"Please?" He nuzzled her stomach. Kissed one hip bone then the other. "Please what?"

She lifted her hips in a silent plea. "You know…you know what I want…"

He nodded, his silky hair rubbing against the tips of her breasts, causing them to tighten even further. "Tell me."

Tell me.

It was what he'd said only minutes before.

Tell me you feel the same way. Tell me it's the same for you.

He wanted everything. Her thoughts and feelings. Her confession.

And in that moment, she'd give him anything he wanted. Whatever he asked.

"Taste me," she whispered, her voice shaky with need, rough with desire.

Shifting back, he slid his arms under her thighs, lifted her to his mouth and, with his eyes on hers, he licked her, a long sweep of his tongue against her core. "Mmm," he murmured. "So sweet."

And then he gently spread her with his fingers, bent his head, and feasted.

He worked her with his tongue, the light scrape of his teeth, until she writhed beneath him. Worked her until pleasure built, strong and steady, until she reached the precipice, only to back off, kissing her inner thighs, whirling his tongue around her center. Again and again he brought her right to the edge of pleasure. Again and again he backed off.

She went wild, her body heated and flushed, sweat coating her skin as she moved beneath him until he gave her what she wanted, what she needed, licking and sucking until she splintered into a thousand pieces. He soothed her with soft kisses, long, slow licks as she came down, her fingers uncurling from the mattress, her arms and legs boneless.

He laid beside her, his erection, thick and hard and long, pressed against the side of her leg, and she rolled over, straddling his chest. Stretched his arms overhead, curling his fingers over the edge of the mattress.

"Don't let go," she told him.

Then with a grin that promised payback, she shifted back until the tip of his cock nudged her opening. She rubbed against him—once, twice, three times—then took him in, her inner core squeezing around him.

Placing her palms on his chest, feeling his heartbeat strong and a bit unsteady beneath her hands, she seated herself fully on him then lifted. Down and up. A slow, languid lovemaking that had her body coming alive once again, had lust coiling through her system when moments ago it had been slackened.

She scraped her nails over his nipples lightly and he shuddered. His arms twitched and started to lower.

She stopped. Shook her head. "Don't let go."

Only after he'd taken hold of the mattress once again did she start to move, taking him deeper. Her fingers curled into his chest, her nails digging into his skin. He met her thrusts, quickened the pace with the force of his pumping hips. Bending down, she kissed him hungrily, dragging her nipples across his smooth chest, holding on to his shoulders so she could go even faster. Harder. Until once again her orgasm built.

She pushed herself upright to take him as far as she could. Spine arched, hands in her own hair, she moved her hips furiously until he tipped his head back, the tendons in his neck tight and sticking out in sharp relief. She watched his face as he came with a shout, his release setting off her own, and she rode him as hard, as fast as she could, milking the pleasure he gave her for all she was worth.

And when she collapsed on top of him, gasping for breath, her body trembling with the aftershocks of her orgasm, his hands smoothing over her back, his mouth trailing across her shoulder, the side of her neck, she knew she was in serious trouble.

Because she was the one who wasn't going to be able to let go.

9

THE MAN KNEW how to cook.

It was unbelievable. Incomprehensible.

And totally and completely unfair.

Sitting at her kitchen table, Quinn glared at Xander's back while he expertly flipped pancakes at her stove.

He cooked, and he did it in only a pair of low-slung running shorts, all the better to tempt her with his washboard abs, those wide shoulders and well-defined arms. Between cracking eggs and scooping out the flour and sugar for the pancakes, he stopped periodically to refill her coffee cup. Told her stories about BUD/S training, the special sort of hell all SEAL candidates had to go through. Talked about his nephews and how his sister had loved the gift certificate to the spa. How he'd gone back and bought one for his mom, just because.

Just because.

Could he get any more perfect?

And before all of that, after the most intense sexual experiences of her life when she was a boneless puddle on her bed, wondering if she'd ever walk again, he'd carried her into the shower and washed every inch of her, including her hair. It hadn't taken long before his soap-slicked hands had worked their magic and she'd come again, the orgasm leaving her a breathless, weak-kneed mess.

Then he'd wrapped her in a towel and deposited her on the edge of the bed before ducking back into the shower to wash himself.

Where he'd sang "Living on a Prayer." Loudly. And so badly she'd wanted to dig her eardrums out of her head and throw them away.

She'd found it endearing nonetheless.

No doubt about it. Whoever was running things really had it in for her.

He set a stack of pancakes in front of her.

If they tasted even halfway decent, she was going to stab him with her fork.

She took a small bite. Shut her eyes on a groan.

Delicious.

Well, that settled it. He truly was perfect.

She was going to have to keep him forever.

The thought had her choking. She coughed, held up her hand when he whirled around, looking like he was ready to jump into action-hero mode and perform the Heimlich maneuver.

"I'm okay," she said between coughs. "Just…went down the…wrong way."

She sipped her coffee and cleared her throat. God, she'd lost her mind. Maybe all those orgasms had damaged a few too many brain cells. She was not keeping Lieutenant Xander Bennett of the navy SEALs. He had a life back East. A career. A future she was sure he had all mapped out, complete with goals, subgoals, timelines and a color-coordinated chart to keep him on track.

A future he hadn't once mentioned her being a part of.

"These are good," she said when he joined her at her

tiny table. "I hadn't realized they taught the culinary arts at Annapolis."

"This is my mom's recipe," he said, adding a scant amount of syrup to his pancakes. Cut a piece off and took a bite. "She worked a lot so she taught us all how to cook. Said it was her duty to make sure we could take care of ourselves."

Quinn had forgotten that his father had passed away when Xander was young. That he and his brother and sister had been raised by a single mother, too. "Do you remember your dad?"

"A little." Frowning thoughtfully, he took a sip of his coffee. "Images of him more than actual memories. What about you?"

"Mine isn't dead," she said, shooting for flippant. "Last I heard, he was alive and well and living with wife number four somewhere in Texas."

"How old were you when your folks split up?"

Her folks hadn't split up. Her dad had left. Walked out one day and just…didn't return. "Eight," she said, hating how just thinking about it, talking about it could drag her right back to that time. "And yes, I remember him. I remember him leaving and I remember waiting, day after day, for him to come home."

Xander covered her hand with his. "I'm sorry."

She forced a shrug. Slid her hand out from under his to take a bite of pancake she didn't want or have the appetite for. "It was a long time ago."

"The pain of losing someone never goes away."

"I didn't lose him. Not like you lost your dad. He left. It didn't matter that he'd made a promise to my mom, that he had a responsibility to me… He chose to leave. I think that's part of the reason why I stayed with Peter for so long," she told him, admitting the truth she'd never dared speak out loud before. Had never been brave enough to fully face. "To prove I'm better than my father. That once I give my word, I keep it."

"What was the other part?"

"It was safe," she said simply. "Don't get me wrong. It sucked, knowing I couldn't trust him, knowing he lied and cheated and would do it again, but with Peter at least I knew the bills were paid, that things were taken care of. It wasn't until I realized that he'd never loved me, that he'd only wanted me so he could dress me up and show me off to his friends and business clients that I was able to leave."

And she hated that it had taken her so long. That she'd traded in her pride and her happiness for security.

"The more I know about him," Xander said in a quiet, dangerous tone, "the more I want to meet him."

She smiled. "More like you want to practice a few of those deadly ninja SEAL moves on him."

"I'd say he deserves it, but he already got what he deserved."

"What's that?"

"He lost you."

Oh. My.

She'd been right, back in her bed, when she'd been reeling from their lovemaking. She wasn't going to be able to let him go.

Not without her heart breaking in the process.

QUINN GOT QUIET, the expression on her face, in her eyes, setting Xander back.

"You okay?" he asked, wondering why she looked so freaked out suddenly. So frightened.

She smiled but it didn't reach her eyes. "Fine." Standing quickly, she grabbed her mug and walked to the counter, poured more coffee into it even though it was already mostly full. "You know, it just occurred to me that I'm monopolizing quite a bit of your time."

His eyes narrowed. *Shit.* He didn't like the sound of this or the way she wouldn't meet his eyes, how her tone had a "this is the end" quality to it.

This wasn't the end of them. Not by a long shot.

"I'm where I want to be," he told her quietly. Honestly. "Who I want to be with."

If anything, that made her look more panicked. "Your mother is probably wondering why you're not around more. And your sister. And Zane," she added, her voice rising as if the louder she spoke, the truer it would make her words. "I'm sure you don't get back to town very often. This is a chance for you to see your brother or your friends."

"My mom isn't wondering anything." He'd already been to more family dinners this trip then he had in the past five years combined. "She's fine. Kerri's fine and Zane's busy with his own life." Truth be told, Zane had done his own disappearing act, showing up for meals or the occasional drop-in at their mom's then taking off again. "And I just saw my friends at the reunion registration. Will be with them at the parade and the reunion."

But the reunion was coming up quickly, which meant his time in Little Creek and his time with Quinn was ending.

"Come with me," he said.

"I'm not big on parades. Besides, the reunion committee already asked me to get my homecoming crown out of storage and play queen again. I declined."

"Not the parade." He didn't even want to think about the parade—or that giant panther float. "The reunion. Come with me."

He wanted her with him. Not to win some challenge, but because he'd be leaving soon afterwards and he wanted her by his side before he did. Wanted to spend as much time with her as possible.

"I'm working that night," she reminded him.

"Then I'll skip the reunion. Spend the night with you at Myer's."

"You can't skip it. You and Zane are the guests of honor."

He shrugged. "Zane'll be there. They don't need both of us."

"I'm pretty sure they do. And won't Zane be upset if you don't show?"

"He won't care."

He'd kick Xander's ass—deservedly—but it'd be worth it.

She shifted. Set her cup down. Picked it up again. "Look, this has been great—"

"This?"

"Yeah. You. Me." She waved between them. "*This*. But we both have so much going on right now—you with your family and friends and all the reunion activities and me with my job and studies…" This time she set her cup down with a decisive snap. "I think it's best, for both of us, if we…back up a little bit. Slow down."

"No."

"Excuse me?"

"No, it's not best. For either of us."

She sent him a flinty look. "I know what's best for me."

"This isn't." He stood, crossed to her and took her gently by the shoulders. "Don't try to end this, Quinn. End us." He grinned down at her, rubbed his thumbs over her skin. "Things are just getting interesting."

She rolled her eyes then snorted out a laugh. "Okay, I'll give you that. But as interesting as it's become, it's still temporary. And I don't see the point in dragging it out."

The point was giving him time so he could persuade

her to make it not so temporary. For him to convince her to give them a chance at making this work. Building something real and long-lasting between them.

But he couldn't tell her that. She was too gun-shy. Was already trying to push him away. If he moved too fast, if he asked for too much, too soon, she'd bolt.

He settled one hand on her hip and brushed her hair aside with the other so he could press his mouth to the side of her neck. "The point is that I'm not ready to let you go. I haven't gotten my fill of you," he murmured. "There are still so many things I want to do to you. So many ways I want to have you."

He darted his tongue out, tasting the saltiness of her skin, and she shivered and grabbed his waist. Pulled him closer, his growing erection nestled against the softness of her belly. "I suppose I could let you hang around another day or two. Just until you run out of ideas."

He raised his head so he could meet her eyes. "Sounds fair. But I should warn you, I have a very active and expansive imagination."

"That so?" She brushed her fingers over his cock. Grinned at his hissed-out breath. "Prove it."

Now, that was a challenge he could gladly accept.

10

QUINN REFILLED HER COFFEE CUP then sat back at her table. She had the afternoon off—which was a good thing as afternoons weren't exactly rush time at Myer's. Plus, staying home gave her time to focus on her studies.

Not that she was. Studying, that was. She should be. She had a paper due and an exam she needed to buckle down for, but when she opened her laptop, the window was open to a shopping site.

Biting her lower lip, she considered the dress on the screen. It was a deep blue, slinky with just enough sparkle. Perfect for a has-been queen.

Perfect for attending her ten-year high school reunion.

She added it to her online shopping bag, picked two-day shipping and tried not to cry as she thought of the damage it was doing to her pitiful savings account, but there you had it. She pushed Order, put in her credit-card information and slammed the laptop lid shut, her heart racing like she'd just run a race.

She was doing it. She was going to her class reunion.

Not because she wanted to be there, necessarily. She was going for Xander.

Taking her coffee with her, she went into the living

room and curled up on her couch to stare out the window. He hadn't asked her to accompany him again. This was her way of surprising him. She wanted to go with him.

Wanted to spend as much time as possible with him while she still could.

Their time together was dwindling fast. Too fast. In a matter of days he'd be gone. And if going to a reunion together and giving people the crazy idea that they were a real couple meant being able to spend a few more hours with him?

She'd take it.

Sipping her coffee, she watched a car pull up and park. A moment later, a pretty blonde got out. When the blonde headed straight for Quinn's door, a bakery box in her hand, Quinn straightened. A moment later, there was a knock on the door.

What was up with that?

Too curious not to find out, Quinn answered the door.

"Hi," the blonde said, with a warm smile. "I'm Vivian. I was hoping we could chat." She lifted the box. "I brought cupcakes."

And now Quinn was even more curious.

And she wouldn't mind a cupcake.

She returned the other woman's friendly grin hesitantly remembering what curiosity did to the cat. "Hi, Vivian." She glanced at the box then up into the woman's face. "Why?"

"First, because I love your boots and figure any woman who has such great taste in footwear is one I'd like to know. Second, I know you grew up here, but you haven't been back long so I thought maybe you could use a friend. And third," she lifted the lid to show off the variety pack of cupcakes, "some things are better discussed with sugar."

"A friend?" She hadn't had a girlfriend since high

school, and even then, she'd been more popular, more liked
for her looks than for her personality. "Let's not be hasty."

The woman's smile remained. "Well, let's focus on that
third reason, because I really, really need to talk to you."

Oh, Quinn didn't like the sound of that. She almost told
her to get lost, that whatever she had to say Quinn wasn't
interested in hearing, but there was something about the
other woman's face, something that told Quinn she wasn't
playing a game.

Crap.

"In that case," Quinn said, opening the door wide and
holding out her arm, "come on in."

Quinn nodded at the table and Vivian sat. She opened
the lid of the box. "Help yourself."

Inside were half a dozen cupcakes. Quinn chose a
chocolate one with mile-high, dark chocolate frosting.
"So what do I owe the honor of having the best baker in
town deliver cupcakes to my door?"

Vivian blinked. "You know who I am?"

Quinn shrugged. "Small town. You're Mike Harris's
sister."

Vivian's mouth turned down. "At the moment I've dis-
owned him, but I suppose, technically, you could say I'm
his sister. Anyway," she continued with a shake of her
head, "I hate to be the bearer of bad news and all that, and
this might sound crazy seeing as how we don't know each
other, but women should stick together, don't you think?"

Quinn was fascinated by the way Vivian talked, quick
and bright, barely taking a breath. "Sisterhood for life,"
she agreed, then took a bite of her cupcake.

Vivian smiled and seemed to relax. "Anyway, I recently
discovered that I have been the consolation prize in a stupid, immature bet."

"Consolation prize?"

Vivian nodded. "Runner-up. Second place. First to lose, as the SEALs say."

"SEALs? Please tell me you're talking about the marine animals."

"Nope," she said. "Afraid not. And while I was the consolation prize, I thought it was only fair to let you know that you were the grand prize."

Everything within Quinn froze. "What?"

"Yeah. Pretty sucky, right? It was a challenge. To see who could get you—Xander or Zane."

"What?" Quinn repeated, softer but with more venom, which her new buddy recognized.

"Don't kill the messenger. I just… I thought you should know."

Quinn realized that the other woman had been hurt by this. It made her own pain easier to deal with, knowing she wasn't alone.

"Men suck," Quinn said, taking a huge bite of the cupcake.

"Amen to that, sister," Vivian said, toasting her with her own cupcake. "So, what are you going to do?"

Quinn considered that question. She'd trusted Xander. Had been contemplating putting her heart on the line for him—*had* put her heart on the line. Had opened up to him only to find out none of it was real.

It hurt. It hurt so much worse than anything Peter had done. Worse than having her father walk out on her.

"I'm going to do what I should have done in the first place," she said quietly. "I'm going to walk away."

XANDER POUNDED ON Quinn's door. He didn't understand it. He knew she was home, he saw her lights on, but she wasn't answering the door.

Two more minutes and he was going to break in.

He knocked again and finally he heard the click of the dead bolt unlocking. The door opened.

He frowned at Quinn, still in jeans and a T-shirt, the same outfit he assumed she'd worn to work. "Are you okay?"

"Other than having a maniac knocking on my door at 3:00 a.m.?" she asked coolly. "I'm fine."

He narrowed his eyes. Something was up. "I waited for you. After work," he clarified.

"Did you?" She shrugged. "I guess you wasted your time."

And she started to shut the door.

He pressed his hand against it, holding it open. "What's wrong?"

"Nothing. I've just decided to take myself out of the running."

"The running?"

She tipped her head to the side, and though there was definitely a lot of anger in her expression, beyond that, he saw hurt in her eyes. "The running as top prize for your little dare."

She knew about the challenge.

Shit.

"It wasn't a dare," he said quietly. "It was a stupid challenge. It didn't mean anything."

She laughed harshly. "No? Seemed to me it meant enough, was important enough for you to win that you came after me. Well, congrats. I hope it was worth it."

She tried to shut the door but he held on. "Worth what?"

"Worth losing me."

It wasn't, he realized. Nothing was worth that. "I didn't come after you because of the challenge. You know that. It was stupid. Meaningless. And I didn't even win," he hurried on. "It wasn't a dare to get you into bed. Just to take you to the reunion—which you refused to do. I lost and I'm glad. I got something so much better," he told her honestly.

"I don't believe you. You told me you don't lie, but you lied to me."

He was losing her. And this time he wasn't sure he could stop it. "Let me in, Quinn," he said softly, taking a chance and touching her—just her arm. His finger trailing over her skin. "Let me in so I can explain."

But she shook her head, looking so hurt it tore him up inside. "Anything you say will be a lie. Now let go of my door before I decide to try out some of my new defensive moves on you."

He hesitated, but it was late and she was obviously upset and he didn't want to make it worse.

If that was even possible.

Letting go of the door, he stepped back, his hands held up in surrender. "This isn't over."

"It really is." She started shutting the door only to stop. Looked at him in a way that made him feel like something smelly under her shoe. "You know the worst part? I trusted you. I knew I shouldn't but you were so convincing. I trusted you," she repeated, "so I guess I have no one to blame for this but myself. Goodbye, Xander."

She shut the door, leaving him on her dark doorstep. Leaving him to face the truth.

The only person to blame was him.

11

THE NIGHT OF the reunion, Quinn was behind the bar at Myer's when Xander walked in looking like a freaking dream in dark dress pants and a crisp white shirt opened at the collar. Her heart tripped.

She'd missed him the past two days. She'd missed him so much.

The bastard.

He headed straight for her. She considered running away but the man was a SEAL.

If he wanted to find her, to catch her, he would.

And she wasn't giving him the satisfaction of letting him know how much he'd hurt her. She'd slipped the other night. Had been raw and vulnerable but now she was stronger. Smarter.

"What'll it be, sailor?" she asked, making sure her voice was a husky purr.

"We need to talk."

Pouring two shots of tequila, she raised her eyebrows. "You know what? I'm all talked out. Oh, I know, you want to talk about me accompanying you to the reunion? Winning that dare?"

"It wasn't a dare," he said through his clenched teeth.

Glad to see she wasn't the only one getting irritated. "It was a challenge. And I don't want to win it." He leaned forward, lowered his voice, his gaze intense. "I want you."

She wanted so badly to believe him.

Stupid, stupid girl.

"Well, you've already had me," she said. "Let someone else have a turn."

The guy at the end of the bar raised his hand. "Where do I sign up for this?"

Xander whirled around and glared, and the guy slunk down on his bar stool. "We're talking," he said, turning back to Quinn. "Now."

"No, I'm working. And you are leaving." She handed the shots to her customers, who were watching the little drama with huge eyes. "Now."

She turned her back on him, and that was her mistake. Not that he couldn't have easily taken her out but she made it too easy for him.

She wouldn't make that mistake again.

So when he leaped over the bar—which she wished she could have seen—and bent down, tossing her over his shoulder, she didn't hesitate. She fought. Kicking and punching the best she could. When Steve said something to Xander, tried to stop him, Xander growled and poor Steve backed up so fast, he knocked over a tower of glasses.

"Dianne is going to kill you," Quinn said gleefully. If only her boss was there right now. "More damages to pay for."

He stalked down the hallway as if he knew where he was going, turned right and stepped into the tiny closet Dianne called her office and shut the door, then set Quinn on her feet, holding on to her upper arms.

She shook her hair from her eyes. "Let me go."

"Not until I've had my say."

"What makes you think I care to hear what you have to say? What makes you think you deserve my time and attention?"

"Nothing," he said simply. "But I'm hoping you'll listen anyway."

She didn't want to. Told herself she couldn't care less about what he had to say but she found herself crossing her arms and muttering, "Fine. Two minutes."

"I'm sorry."

She waited but that seemed to be the extent of it. "If I'd known you were going to be that succinct," she said drily. "I would have given you two seconds."

She tried to get by but he blocked her. "I'm sorry I hurt you."

"I'm fine," she said quickly.

"You were right. I did lie to you, but not about what you think. Not about my feelings for you. The only reason I accepted that challenge was because it gave me a reason to approach you. I knew Zane would try to win it no matter what, and I couldn't stand the thought of seeing the two of you together."

"That makes no sense."

"It does. I had a crush on you. In high school."

Her eyes widened and she was surprised at the depth of pain his confession brought. "That's what this whole thing was about?" she asked. "You living out some teenage fantasy?"

"Yes. No." He shook his head. Stabbed his fingers through his hair. "I had a crush on you, but it wasn't real. You're real. The person you are now— Quinn, you're amazing. Smart and strong and so beautiful. I don't want to lose you. I'm falling in love with you."

His words went right to her heart. Her breath caught and

she stumbled back a step. "No. No, it's too late. I'm not that girl. I told you that before. I'm not a princess. I'm just me."

He nodded. "I know. You are who I want. Give me another chance. Trust me."

"I can't," she whispered.

His mouth flattened. "You mean you won't."

"Does it matter?"

"It matters that you're too afraid to take a chance. Stop playing it safe," he said. "Stop living this half-life where you keep yourself so guarded and distant from everyone and everything. Take a chance on me." He stepped forward and touched her cheek. "Take a chance on us. We can make it work."

But she was too scared. She stepped back. "It's too late."

He stiffened. "You got what you wanted."

"What do you mean?"

"This. You've been waiting for me to screw up, to catch me in a lie or to let you down in some way so you'd have an excuse to walk away from me. You got what you wanted," he repeated softly. "I just hope it's what you can live with."

He opened the door and stepped out into the hall, shutting the door behind him. Leaving her alone. She knew he was right. This was what she'd wanted. What she'd expected.

And she couldn't live with it. Didn't want to.

XANDER STOOD NEXT to the piano at the country club while "Fergalicious" played over the loudspeakers. People danced and talked, a few hanging around the buffet table, more hanging out at the bar. The room was filled with balloons, streamers and enough paper panthers to fill a damn jungle.

People kept their distance from him—probably because when anyone got too close, he glared at them until they scurried away. He wasn't in the party mood. Had been paraded around—literally, and riding that panther float in the parade down Main Street had been the stuff of nightmares— enough. He just wanted tonight to be over.

Wanted another opportunity to talk to Quinn again. To convince her to forgive him. To give him another chance.

"Yo," Zane said, coming up to Xander. "Great party, right?"

Xander nodded. Something was up with his twin. "You look like hell."

"Thanks, man. Glad to know you've always got my back."

"Always."

The song changed to Beyoncé's "Irreplaceable," and on the dance floor, Mrs. Marshall, their old algebra teacher, did a shimmy and shake against Mr. Bridges, the PE teacher.

Zane went white. "Oh, man."

"So wrong." But Xander couldn't turn away. It was like a car wreck.

"We're supposed to find Kyle," Zane said.

"Right." Xander sighed. "Challenge time, and all that."

"Yeah. All that." Zane frowned. "You okay?"

Great. Now he had Zane wondering what the hell was going on with him. "Why wouldn't I be?"

"Can I ask you something?"

As long as it wasn't about him, Xander was game. Still, Zane didn't come to him for advice. He followed his own path. "You want my advice? Did you bump your head?"

"Challenge time!"

Both he and Zane looked over as Kyle held his hand up.

Xander glanced at Zane and they both stood there, leaving Kyle's bid for a high five unanswered.

Lenny slapped Kyle's hand then turned to Xander and

Zane. "So which one of you is here with Quinn? I've got twenty riding on this. If I can collect before the next song, I can snag a date for the rest of the party."

Kyle shook his hand. Lenny always had been an aggressive slapper. "Who scored?"

Xander held his breath, letting it out only when Zane made a zero with his hand. "Not me."

Xander shrugged. No way was he telling these guys about him and Quinn. "I'm here alone."

He let their chatter, their gripes and complaints swirl around him. He didn't give a shit what they thought, if they concluded he and Zane were losing their edge.

He never should have agreed to the challenge in the first place.

Kyle held up his hand to silence the group. "Okay, so neither of you could bring in the win. But we have to declare a winner. So who was closest to a date tonight?"

"Cupcake," Lenny said. "Zane scored a cupcake."

But when Xander glanced at his brother, expecting to see triumph on his face at winning, he was surprised. Zane didn't look triumphant. He looked determined.

And he was staring at someone bringing in a cake.

He clapped Xander on the shoulder with enough force to have Xander catching his balance. "Gotta go," he said. "I've got a lady to see about a cake."

He took off, all of their friends watching him, but not Xander. He couldn't. His gaze was glued to the entrance. And to Quinn, walking straight toward him.

THE DRESS HAD gotten here in time, Quinn thought as she walked through the crowded ballroom. It was a sea of school colors, filled with people she'd known her entire life. But there was only one person she wanted to talk to.

"You win," she blurted when she reached Xander. "And you were right."

He didn't take her in his arms, which drove her crazy, but at least he wasn't walking away from her. "What was I right about?"

She licked her lips, ignored his buddies standing around as they glanced at them and then away at whatever was going on in the center of the room. "About me. You were right. I did want you to screw up. I expected it and it made it easier for me to end things between us. That way I could blame you without taking responsibility for my own choices. For not…for not being brave enough to take a chance on life."

He stilled. "What do I win?" he asked, his soft words somehow reaching her over the cheers and catcalls that suddenly filled the room.

She swallowed. "You win me," she breathed. "Not that I'm any sort of prize."

He finally stepped forward and pulled her slowly into his arms. "You're the best prize. The only one I want."

He kissed her, and when he lifted his head, he turned, and she followed his gaze to the reason everyone else was whooping and hollering. Zane, with his arms around Vivian, in the center of the room.

The brothers grinned at each other, then Xander turned back and kissed Quinn again.

"You in for an adventure?" he asked when he was done, his lips close to her ear.

She leaned back so she could meet his eyes. Touched his cheek. "I'm all in."

* * * * *

Harlequin is thrilled to announce
the launch of a new sexy, contemporary
digital-only series in January 2018!
With the exciting launch of this new
series, June 2017 will be the last month of
publication for Harlequin® Blaze® books.

For more passionate stories, indulge in these fun,
sexy reads with the irresistible heroes you can't
get enough of!

HARLEQUIN *Presents*®

Glamorous international settings...
powerful men...passionate romances.

HARLEQUIN *Desire*

Powerful heroes...scandalous secrets...
burning desires.

If you enjoy passionate stories from Harlequin® Blaze®, you will love Harlequin® Presents!

Do you want alpha males, decadent glamour and jet-set lifestyles? Step into the sensational, sophisticated world of Harlequin® Presents, where sinfully tempting heroes ignite a fierce and wickedly irresistible passion!

Look for eight new stories every month!
Recommended Read for July 2017

Maisey Yates The Prince's Captive Virgin Ruthless prince Adam Katsaros offers Belle a deal—he'll release her father if she becomes his mistress! Adam's gaze awakens a heated desire in Belle. Her innocent beauty might redeem his royal reputation—but can she tame the beast inside?

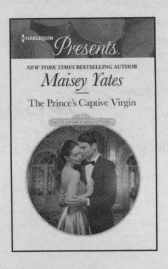

Look out for The Secret Billionaires trilogy from Harlequin® Presents!

Three extraordinary men accept the challenge of leaving their billionaire lifestyles behind. But in *Salazar's One-Night Heir* by Jennifer Hayward, Alejandro must also seek revenge for a decades-old injustice…

Tycoon Alejandro Salazar will take any opportunity to expose the Hargrove family's crime against his—including accepting a challenge to pose as their stable groom! His goal in sight, Alejandro cannot allow himself to be distracted by the gorgeous Hargrove heiress…

Her family must pay, yet Alejandro can't resist innocent Cecily's fiery passion. And when their one night of bliss results in an unexpected pregnancy, Alejandro will legitimize his heir and restore his family's honor…by binding Cecily to him with a diamond ring!

Don't miss

The Secret Billionaires
SALAZAR'S ONE-NIGHT HEIR

by Jennifer Hayward Available July 2017!

*Ariston Kavakos makes impoverished Keeley Turner a
proposition: a month's employment on his island, at his
command. Soon her resistance to their sizzling chemistry
weakens! But when there's a consequence, Ariston makes
one thing clear: Keeley will become his bride…*

Read on for a sneak preview of
Sharon Kendrick's book
THE PREGNANT KAVAKOS BRIDE

ONE NIGHT WITH CONSEQUENCES
Conveniently wedded, passionately bedded!

"You're offering to buy my baby? Are you out of your
mind?"

"I'm giving you the opportunity to make a fresh start."

"Without my baby?"

"A baby will tie you down. I can give this child everything
it needs," Ariston said, deliberately allowing his gaze to drift
around the dingy little room. "You cannot."

"Oh, but that's where you're wrong, Ariston," Keeley
said, her hands clenching. "You might have all the houses
and yachts and servants in the world, but you have a great
big hole where your heart should be—and therefore you're
incapable of giving this child the thing it needs more than
anything else!"

"Which is?"

"Love!"

Ariston felt his body stiffen. He loved his brother
and once he'd loved his mother, but he was aware of his
limitations. No, he didn't do the big showy emotion he

suspected she was talking about, and why should he, when he knew the brutal heartache it could cause? Yet something told him that trying to defend his own position was pointless. She would fight for this child, he realized. She would fight with all the strength she possessed, and that was going to complicate things. Did she imagine he was going to accept what she'd just told him and play no part in it? Politely dole out payments and have sporadic weekend meetings with his own flesh and blood? Or worse, no meetings at all? He met the green blaze of her eyes.

"So you won't give this baby up and neither will I," he said softly. "Which means that the only solution is for me to marry you."

He saw the shock and horror on her face.

"But I don't want to marry you! It wouldn't work, Ariston—on so many levels. You must realize that. Me, as the wife of an autocratic control freak who doesn't even like me? I don't think so."

"It wasn't a question," he said silkily. "It was a statement. It's not a case of if you will marry me, Keeley—just when."

"You're mad," she breathed.

He shook his head. "Just determined to get what is rightfully mine. So why not consider what I've said, and sleep on it and I'll return tomorrow at noon for your answer—when you've calmed down. But I'm warning you now, Keeley—that if you are willful enough to try to refuse me, or if you make some foolish attempt to run away and escape—" he paused and looked straight into her eyes "—I will find you and drag you through every court in the land to get what is rightfully mine."

Don't miss
THE PREGNANT KAVAKOS BRIDE
available July 2017 wherever
Harlequin Presents® books and ebooks are sold.

www.Harlequin.com

HARLEQUIN®

A *Romance* FOR EVERY MOOD™

Love the Harlequin book you just read?

Your opinion matters.

Review this book on your favorite book site, review site, blog or your own social media properties and share your opinion with other readers!

HARLEQUIN®

A *Romance* FOR EVERY MOOD™

JUST CAN'T GET ENOUGH?

Join our social communities
and talk to us online.

You will have access to the latest
news on upcoming titles and special
promotions, but most importantly,
you can talk to other fans about your
favorite Harlequin reads.

Harlequin.com/Community

Facebook.com/HarlequinBooks

Twitter.com/HarlequinBooks

Pinterest.com/HarlequinBooks